The Imperative Truth

Craig Miller

Ukiyoto Publishing

All global publishing rights are held by

Ukiyoto Publishing

Published in 2024

Content Copyright © Craig Miller

ISBN 9789362690630

All rights reserved.

No part of this publication may be reproduced, transmitted, or stored in a retrieval system, in any form by any means, electronic, mechanical, photocopying, recording or otherwise, without the prior permission of the publisher.

The moral rights of the author have been asserted.

This is a work of fiction. Names, characters, businesses, places, events, locales, and incidents are either the products of the author's imagination or used in a fictitious manner. Any resemblance to actual persons, living or dead, or actual events is purely coincidental.

This book is sold subject to the condition that it shall not by way of trade or otherwise, be lent, resold, hired out or otherwise circulated, without the publisher's prior consent, in any form of binding or cover other than that in which it is published.

www.ukiyoto.com

Contents

Chapter 1	1
Chapter 2	5
Chapter 3	8
Chapter 4	12
Chapter 5	15
Chapter 6	23
Chapter 7	26
Chapter 8	34
Chapter 9	36
Chapter 10	40
Chapter 11	43
Chapter 12	49
Chapter 13	52
Chapter 14	55
Chapter 15	61
Chapter 16	63
Chapter 17	68
Chapter 18	71
Chapter 19	74
Chapter 20	76
Chapter 21	80
Chapter 22	85
Chapter 23	88
Chapter 24	92

Chapter 25	95
Chapter 26	98
Chapter 27	101
Chapter 28	103
Chapter 29	109
Chapter 30	112
Chapter 31	115
Chapter 32	117
Chapter 33	121
Chapter 34	128
Chapter 35	131
Chapter 36	134
Chapter 37	139
Chapter 38	142
Chapter 39	148
Chapter 40	153
Chapter 41	157
Chapter 42	159
Chapter 43	161
Chapter 44	163
Chapter 45	168
Chapter 46	170
Chapter 47	172
Chapter 48	176
Chapter 49	179
Chapter 50	182

Chapter 51	184
Chapter 52	189
Chapter 53	193
Chapter 54	201
Chapter 55	203
Chapter 56	206
Chapter 57	209
Chapter 58	211
Chapter 59	215
Chapter 60	217
Chapter 61	219
Chapter 62	224
Chapter 63	227
Chapter 64	232
Chapter 65	235
Chapter 66	239
Chapter 67	242
Chapter 68	244
Chapter 69	250
Chapter 70	252
Chapter 71	260
Chapter 72	266
Chapter 73	269
Chapter 74	271
Chapter 75	274
Chapter 76	277

Chapter 77	282
Chapter 78	287
Chapter 79	290
Chapter 80	292
Chapter 81	296
Chapter 82	299
Chapter 83	304
Chapter 84	306
Chapter 85	308
Chapter 86	311
Chapter 87	313
About the Author	*315*

2007

Chapter 1

"North Korea's newspapers have more freedom than our paper."

The school's superintendent, Mr. Gensen—demonstrator of Lakewood High discipline—looks unamused at my proclamation. His head's bald and I smelled his leather cowboy boots before entering his office.

"The issue to why you're here, Mr. McCarthy, is your article 'Stand Up for Your Team.'" He waves the latest issue of *Lakewood High Bi-Weekly* in front of me like I've never seen our school newspaper, written for it for two years, and been in Writing in Print my entire junior year. (Don't look at me; I didn't choose the name of the class.)

"I don't see the problem." All I did was write about how we should be allowed to show school spirit (ironic if you knew me, yes) during our hockey games—the *only* sport our school is remotely good at. Really, kids learn to skate before they learn to crawl around these parts in Muskegon, Michigan.

"And, yes, maybe you don't have some of the same *freedom* as other newspapers." He sounds like the word *freedom* pains him. "But you need to be more conscientious of our school image. You need to be more sensitive to the needs of others, Mr. McCarthy," Mr. Gensen loves repeating my name.

"Who complained?"

"That's not the issue here." A bunch of senior citizens yelled at us the previous game when we stood. Their legs probably couldn't handle it. I understand this, but maybe they shouldn't go to games. Maybe they should sit at home and watch Jeopardy or go to Hospice where they belong.

I cough.

I recall my first day of Writing in Print with Mr. Cannon.

"Journalism is founded on the principal of reporting facts," Mr. Cannon said. "Journalism can be viewed as the fourth pillar of government. This means when the government or other companies are doing anything shady, journalists can report it to the general public. Here in the United States, we have freedom of the press, unlike other countries. The government can tell a news organization they don't *want* them to publish something, but ultimately, that choice is left to the newspaper. But with that being said, we are in a school and subjected to slightly different standards …" He said the last part a bit quietly, and I doubt anybody in the room heard him.

Mr. Gensen sneers at me. "When respectable members of the community like Mrs. Bassett complain, we have a duty to uphold."

He sounds like he's reading out of a Manual titled, "How to Be a Complete Douche-bag."

"I knew it was her!" It's not a *coincidence* that Henry Bassett who couldn't even skate made the varsity hockey team or that now I'm being called to the office. It's all about their goddamn image.

"It's all politics. Got it." I'm not going to let him bullshit me.

"Don't for one second think politics has anything to do with this." A vein in his head bulges and he clenches his teeth together.

I smile.

"May I remind you, this is not your first warning Mr. McCarthy."

In the fall, the varsity soccer coach punished the team for making condescending comments when he wanted them to pray before a meal. He made the team run Suicides—the drill where they run back and forth from various distances—the entire practice and three kids puked. I pointed out in my article that two members of the team were *Muslim,* so it was ridiculous he made them pray to his Christian "god." Needless to say, the coach expressed dissatisfaction with my article; I got reprimanded and one detention.

"It's only going to get worse from here," Mr. Gensen looks at me predatorily. "Two detentions will be your punishment."

He hands me the slip. I'm supposed to go home and have a parent or legal guardian sign it. I'll forge my Pop's signature, not like I haven't done that over a hundred times.

"I really want you think about how your actions affect those around you, not just the school but the whole community."

"Maybe I'll write my next article on old people encouraging my peers to knit quilts, watch Jeopardy, and hit mailboxes while they dive." I can't hide my sarcasm.

"Make sure there isn't a third time, otherwise there will be stricter consequences," he threatens.

The bell rings, indicating it's time for second hour Sport's Skills—so it's time to hear sexist locker room banter and see my peers naked in the shower. I can't imagine a worse consequence than keeping me in this shithole.

Chapter 2

Anyone who thinks high school is how they portray in the movies where you have your jocks, preps, cheerleaders, nerds, and goths needs to reassess themselves. I mean, sure, there are representations of that, but they're more like caricatures.

And even in the "groups" social flexibility is extremely mobile.

But some kids are assholes.

Take, for example, the kids in my gym class. Younger sophomores. Right now, we're taking our mandatory after-class showers in "Sports Skills." Let me tell you this: there is nothing pleasant about being required to shower with a bunch of guys with no barriers, genitalia flopping. It probably isn't much different than a prison.

But then I think about how I don't want to smell bad in my next class.

One of the sophomores, Connor, who's on the hockey team, is squirting shampoo in this skinny freshman's hair while he tries to repeatedly wash it out. Then he throws the bottle to Nick who squirts more shampoo in his hair.

"Guys stop," the freshman pleads.

After the third time, I say, "Jesus Christ, let the kid shower in peace, you assholes."

I say it a little bit louder than I mean to. It echoes throughout the locker room.

They stop and look at me.

Coach Parsons—who also coaches the hockey team and teaches gym class—comes by. While his style of teaching is laid back, he doesn't tolerate bullying. "Is everything alright in here, gentleman?"

"Yes," we answer.

Locker Room Talk comes post-shower. This is where males talk in a bragging manner about their sexual conquests to assert their heterosexuality.

"Did you finally get Jessica to blow you?" Connor asks.

"More than that," Nick, Jessica's boyfriend, says. Nick comments on the state of her vaginal snugness and informs us, "Her blow job skills could be better. She scraped my penis."

"Maybe somebody needs to teach her," Connor says, with a smirk on his face. I can't help but feel the sudden urge to punch him in his nuts. With how Connor talks, over boastful, it makes me wonder if he's *actually* a virgin sometimes, or one of the biggest douchebags at our school. Either way, the choices aren't particularly great: he's fake or simply the type of guy no father would want their daughter to date.

The thing is, I know when these guys are around their girlfriends, they'd *never* talk like this. Instead, they act like good boyfriends and are sweet. They act *nice* even.

In the locker room, they're Neanderthals. The only two topics discussed are parties and sex.

"I'm working on it," Nick says.

As if diverting attention away from himself, Nick looks at me and smiles. Last I knew, we weren't exactly besties. "How are you doing with Carmen?" he asks.

"I don't know what you're talking about," I say. My cheeks redden.

"Are you working on that *still?*" Working on, implies, *trying to gain sexual favors from*. The *still* part implies my lack of courting ability, or the inability to gain sexual favors. Even though it wasn't about that. I don't mention how much I actually liked Carmen.

"Dude, shut up."

"She's flatter than my back anyway," Connor says.

I think ahead to my next class, knowing I'll see Carmen in person and it'll send excitement and pain through me all at once.

Chapter 3

Third hour Physics is my favorite hour of the day because of Carmen. The first day she entered the classroom last semester everything stopped. I felt my atoms drawn to hers. This desire has only grown stronger throughout the school year.

After everything that happened—details I won't go into right now—I still feel something but now there's a sharp pang within and it hurts to breathe.

It didn't end well. Four simple words: *These aren't relationship feelings.*

And here she is acting like none of that ever happened. Wearing high heels and a short jean skirt. Even though it's the middle of *winter*. In Michigan, our winters are Antarctic. Picture the third ice age, except worse. Generally, they span from early November until March, if not April.

Our teacher, Mr. West, is God-awful. He's up there and I swear he's making the shit up as he's explaining it to us, pulling letters and numbers out of his ass. I zone out most of the time, and if it wasn't for John Kenzinger, the kid I sit next to, I would have failed by now. We have an unspoken arrangement: I give him rides home from school. He shares his answers.

"We're going to break off into lab," Mr. West says.

Talk about saving my life.

My lab partners are Kevin and John. Between the two of them, they normally figure out the lab in no time. If it was left up to me, I'd be burning the place down. Not on purpose, of course, but I can't figure out any of the science if it was required to save my goddamn life.

Buck stares at Carmen. Particularly her derriere. He's always super rude, and I don't think he cares for me too much to be honest. Not to mention he stares like a creeper sometimes.

"What are you looking at?" I ask.

The guys at his table laugh. I'm a comedian.

He stutters for a second. Rita, Carmen's friend, comes behind us and says, "Really, what are you looking at, Buck?"

Carmen turns around and looks at him. Buck's cheeks redden.

Don't get me wrong, my mind sometimes goes in the gutter when I think about Carmen, but my problem is that I like her too much.

"Just because you want her and can't have her doesn't mean you need to be an asshole," Buck says.

This hits a little bit too close to home. Carmen and I used to talk *every* single day until it all changed.

"You don't know anything," I say.

If I said I was well-liked at Lakewood High, I would be lying.

I do sometimes find our science labs interesting. But just because I'm intrigued, it doesn't mean it makes sense to me. I can't understand the metric system and why I want to put this amount of fluid in this beaker while lighting the Bunsen burner to a certain degree and write what I observe. I'd rather stare out the window and watch the snowflakes fall. They say each one is different and so unique; why do they all look the same when they fall down?

"Dude, we can't figure this out," Kevin says to me.

"You mean the great Kevin Allen is stumped, and Kenzinger can't help?"

"Come back from la-la land for a bit and help us out." And I know by *help us out* he doesn't mean he wants me to start picking up beakers and experimenting. He means he wants me to find a more competent group on this particular lab and work my magic.

I shrug my shoulders.

"Go ask them," Kevin motions towards Carmen's group. She's partnered with Emily and Rita. I don't like Rita much if we're being honest. When she heard Carmen and I were talking, she asked, "Isn't that kid gay?"

I walk over to Carmen. For a split second, I wonder if it will feel weird, considering everything that happened before.

"Do you notice anything different about me?" I notice how her eyes look even bluer when I'm standing a foot away from her than across the room.

"You shaved." She gives me a weird look.

"No, it's my shoes."

She laughs. "Is that all you really came over here to tell me?"

"Well ... I'm strictly here on business."

"Of course, we don't talk anymore."

"You know why."

She looks at me, deep, searching, and I don't like it.

"I was wondering if we could share answers."

"You mean you want to *cheat*?"

"*Cheat*, no. I was thinking more of a *collaboration*. I want to *borrow* answers."

Carmen looks up at me with her blue eyes and gives me a crooked smile. I remember why I liked her in the first place.

"Thanks," I say as she lowers her paper.

"Your last article was good. How did the administration feel about it?"

"I already got called into the office." The bell rings and I retreat to my seat.

When I go back to my seat to collect my stuff, Buck says, "I didn't realize you two still talked."

I don't say anything as I collect my things. I could say something like, "It's complicated," but I don't.

The only useful thing I've ever learned in Physics: For every action there is an equal and opposite reaction.

Chapter 4

My weekend plans are not strict. They involve slight intoxication, sometimes marijuana, and a little bit of adventure.

When I get home, I have the house to myself. A common occurrence. I double-check just to make sure Pop's car isn't in the garage for some reason; occasionally he makes it home early. I've searched every square inch of this house when he's not home. I've rummaged through the gun safe (the combination is his birthday). His room. (There's nothing of notable interest in his room.)

The liquor cabinet is in the living room by the T.V.

I know it is time for my Friday Afterschool Drink; it has become a solo celebratory ritual for accomplishing another week at Lakewood—or one less week until my graduation.

I never used to drink like this before I met Carmen.

Going to the liquor cabinet, I take a look at the bottles. Because I don't want my father to notice the gradual depletion of his alcohol, I am fastidious about which bottle I select.

This is not like a movie where a guy sits down, loosens his tie and pours his whiskey into a glass and maybe adds ice and contemplates his life. I tried that my first time—just pouring myself a glass of whiskey—and it was goddamn awful. No human being in their right mind would sit here sipping a glass of alcohol for sheer enjoyment.

The truth is it all tastes like shit. There's never been any good tasting alcohol where a person sat down and thought, *I enjoy this*, in the history of alcoholic beverages. It's to feel the intoxicating effects. I prefer not to taste the alcohol. Therefore, mixers became a necessity. I must admit, while the taste is horrible, it can be disguised by orange juice—especially vodka and orange juice—and I enjoy the results of drinking alcohol.

My Pops calls on the house phone. He got me my first cell phone this past Christmas. Not a fancy Razor like most of the kids in my school.

"I am going to be late coming home tonight," he says. "You can fend for yourself for dinner."

"Working late?"

"No."

I don't say anything.

"I have a date."

Since mom disappeared, sometimes I wonder if I derived an inability to woo the ladies from my father. Some type of inherited genetic disorder. My dad's father possesses the same problem. My grandmother left him. She didn't even bother keeping in contact with the rest of the family. She migrated to Florida and nobody's heard from her since.

"Go Pops." After I say it, I wonder if my dad is going to have sex tonight. It's one of those weird things to think about. Obviously, he has done it before, because I'm here. It's just not somewhere I want my mind to go.

I pour myself some vodka and go to the kitchen to grab some orange juice.

Before I even take a sip of my drink, Carmen calls me asking if she can come over because she has some pot in her possession.

Chapter 5

Since becoming a part-time stoner—beginning this year, junior year—I've picked up on terms used and been able to decipher more than was presented to me at D.A.R.E. in my childhood. For example, I know where the choke is on a bowl. I know a bowl is not the reference to the kind old people eat soup from. And the difference between a joint and a blunt is the wrapping paper: a joint being literally paper-like material; the blunt a cigarillo like wrapping. I know what weed looks like and the distinct herbal odor, which slightly reeks. A hard to describe yet distinguishable odor. Fellow kids who indulge claim to distinguish the quality of bud by the smell of it.

I confirmed the party store, Aces, sells bowls to minors. Later I was told to call it a pipe because this implies tobacco rather than marijuana or narcotics, but since I'm underage for tobacco I don't see the point. I simply walked in, asked for a bowl and the guy showed me some. I purchased it without being asked for identification and before I left the owner said, "Make sure you take off the sticker." The sticker that said "Aces" on it.

"I'm surprised. I didn't think you were going to acknowledge me in school again." I state the obvious when she comes over; I'm not sure what I'm trying to get after. Maybe I want to really know *why* it all happened. And I did think we'd *never* talk again.

We went through a phase earlier this semester where we didn't talk for an entire month.

She AIMed me when she missed Physics two weeks ago and we started talking again.

"I thought we were over this." She looks down. I notice her tank top underneath her coat.

Once she told me she had a dream where I shot her—very public at school and it was a whole murder/suicide thing. Another time I dreamed about her sitting on my bed again and she said, "I want to give us a chance." When I woke up, I cried.

We used to talk every day. "I guess you've came around." Although it's not like we *talked* about it.

I don't know all of the rules, and I'm not exactly sure she's keen on it either considering both of us have zero experience in the girlfriend/boyfriend department. But she made it clear our relationship is not in that department anyway.

I usher Carmen upstairs.

She produces the weed in a small plastic bag I doubt most stores sell. Where do drug dealers get such bags?

Carmen takes her glass bowl out of her coat pocket.

"I forgot my manners. I should have offered to put your coat in the closet."

She looks at me like I'm weird. A look I wish I could say I've grown accustomed to but has yet to grow on me.

"I'll just drop it wherever," she says. "Assuming I can find it in your messy room."

She leaves her coat on.

Due to mom being out of the picture, Pops never found it in him to nag about the cleanliness of my room. He'll clean the house and encourages me to partake, which

I reluctantly contribute to at times, but not on a regular basis.

Carmen goes through the ritual of breaking up the weed, using her hands and packs her glass bowl, or "pipe." Purple stripes run down all sides of the bowl.

We each suck in our first hit, experiencing the harshness of the smoke in our lungs, which, of course, is killing us. You're supposed to hold it in as long as you possibly can, but I exhale early due to not wanting to cough and look unmanly in front of Carmen.

After my second hit, the THC produces a very noticeable effect on not only me and my body but my overall perception. My muscles feel like they melted. My physical ability to move slows down and my coordination is off; my thoughts erratic and my cognitive functions diminished.

Being high is *weird*.

"Are all boys' rooms this messy?" Carmen looks around at the clothes on the floor, papers strewn over my messy desk where I do homework and write my articles for the newspaper, the floor dirty and unvacuumed and a few empty glasses scattered about.

"Probably."

She tsks.

"I've never been in your room."

"Why would you want to?" she asks. After a few seconds of silence, she smirks. "Oh, I get it."

I wonder how much she understands. I want to tell her I know I rushed into it all. I want to do it differently. I want to invent a time machine and go back to before this. Be friends first and *then* date.

"The guys in the locker room say you're flat anyway."

"I'm most definitely not flat. Sure, not the most robust, but there are breasts here."

"I believe the phrase used was, *flatter than my back*."

She takes off her coat. "Seriously, feel."

I hesitate.

She uses her telepathic powers. "This isn't a trick. Feel."

My hands move over her breasts, slow at first, then I knead a bit. My first feel of female breasts.

"See," she says. I could spend a great magnitude of time in my future exploring them.

"I guess you're not flat." Not that it would matter if she was.

A warm sensation washes over my body that may not be directly related to the cannabis. I never thought this moment would happen. Let alone Carmen would be in my room again.

We decide to make popcorn because it sounds good.

"It's so weird listening to it pop," Carmen says.

"Many things are weird now."

For a split second, I become self-conscious, and I wonder how Carmen sees me.

"You're so high right now."

"I think we both are."

"It took you forever." Which is true. The first few times I tried it I remained completely stone-cold sober while those around me were staring at the walls and laughing uncontrollably for no particular reason. In a way, this may make smoking pot appear dumb, but it does heighten everything and dull everything at the same time. Later, I was told the delay in it not working is relatively normal for new people experiencing the ganja.

Carmen and I sit on the couch, and my whole body sinks into it.

"This cushion is *so* soft," Carmen observes.

We flip through the channels, but nothing is on.

"Do you remember Penny Normen?" Carmen asks.

"Kind of, why?"

"Just she, you know …"

"Died. I didn't know you were close."

Last year in a car accident. People kept saying things like, "She's in a better place now." But I didn't understand what was so much better about being buried in the ground. Or people said, "God works in mysterious ways." Again, I didn't see what was so mysterious about never graduating high school, finding a job someday, getting married, and eventually having kids.

A cross next to the road is a pretty shitty way of being remembered.

"We weren't," Carmen says. "I don't know why I thought about her. It's just weird. One second you're here, and the next you're not. No warning. You don't even get to graduate."

"I've never had someone close to me die," I say.

"I've only had my grandmother."

"I've never been to a funeral." In fact, nobody I've ever known who has been influential in my life has died and no family members have "passed away" either.

We decide to relocate to the garage. I don't want the whole house to smell like pot when my Pops gets back home. I don't know if he'll necessarily start enforcing strict boundaries, but he will at least *say* something and look at me disapprovingly, wondering if some kind of intervention is necessary so I don't live the rest of my life with him. I would say in our basement, but since we don't have one, it's not possible.

We smoke more and by this time it's completely dark outside. The garage is rarely used at my house. My dad doesn't even *park* in it, which makes no sense in Michigan in the middle of winter, considering the garage would make it so he didn't have to brush off his car every morning. When I asked him if I could park in it, it was a firm "No."

Chips and cheese sound good, and we watch as the cheese melts on the chips as the microwave illuminates them.

Everything sounds like the best idea ever.

"Did you know that Avery Bowen is thinking of running for Snow Coming King?" Carmen asks.

The only open transgender student at Lakewood High.

"I didn't know that. I don't get why." Not that I really care either way.

"Shouldn't we like do something about it, like try to help?"

"You're stoned."

"Just because I'm high as a helium balloon that doesn't mean it's not a good idea." Carmen's eyes look bloodshot. My mouth feels dry, like I have been in the desert for weeks without a drop of water.

"If I don't drink water, I'm going to die," I announce.

"No, you won't."

"I haven't drank water for years."

"Don't try to change the subject."

"I don't even know how we could *help*."

"We can brainstorm."

We forget.

The rest of the night goes by in fast snapshots, and split-second videos—small micro-scenes.

We talk in tongues, mumble words that we can make sense of at the time, we laugh at everything, over what I can't remember, and I can't recall entire conversations. I just know we are incredibly high, which is kind of a weird way of describing it because it feels like a bunch of random neurological firings but the inability to make sense of simple stuff right in front of your face.

We talk and I think all these thoughts, and looking at her, I know she's thinking quite a bit too.

We decide to visit the cemetery.

"Ghosts *are* real," she says.

"Doubtful."

We recognize we are both too impaired to operate a motor vehicle so delay the trip until tomorrow.

Chapter 6

We walk the cemetery. Headstones upon headstones.

Cemeteries are probably the most depressing place a person can be. They are creepy if you think about it—thousands of dead bodies decomposing beneath your feet. My grandpa and my dad already bought their own headstones and plot for where they want to be buried. Tell me this isn't even *more* depressing than the concept of a cemetery—to plan your own goddamn burial while you're still alive. Quite honestly, I don't care what people do when I die. They could throw my body into a river or burn me and spread my ashes all over the place.

It won't matter because I'll be dead.

According to rumor, spirits haunt Nunica cemetery. In fact, it's not just my peers that regard it as the most haunted cemetery around but all of West Michigan.

"Do you believe in magic beans and giants too?" I ask Carmen.

"Ghosts are real," she says for at least the fourth time tonight. "They *have* to be."

She always thinks something *has to be*. When asked to provide logic to back up the reasoning she fails to say anything I'd consider even remotely rationale. This includes topics about the Bible or post-life existence. We'll never agree on this. It's not like I hold some animosity in my heart towards her or any Bible-thumping, pick-up driving inbred who secretly jerks off to incest pictures on Google when his parents are away.

"There's no such thing as ghosts."

"Maybe you just haven't seen one."

"I haven't seen one because they aren't real." Carmen and I could debate for hours.

"How do you explain the stories then, the first-hand experiences?"

"The same way I explain religious ones," I say. "Research's shown tripping on acid produces the same feelings and visuals as a religious experience. The chemicals in our brains trick us. Horror movies and all that don't help."

"That doesn't explain all of it." Carmen is giving me a look that's hard to explain. She focuses directly on me with an arched eyebrow, as if she's trying *too* hard to look sexy like a model, and like she doesn't believe a word I say.

"People lie all the time. They make up stories just like Luke Hanson." (Who I don't mention I noticed by her locker engaging in small talk last week. Not that it matters. I just don't want her to be duped by some loser.)

"Is somebody *jealous*?" Carmen smirks.

"Not at all. In fact, I feel bad for anybody who tries to date you in the future."

Any time we talk about dating, the conversation starts to get uncomfortable or one of us starts to get all butthurt. Most of the time, I'll admit, that someone is usually me.

"You're such a nice guy," she says, sarcasm not even faintly disguised.

We look at each other like we both want to say so much more but don't.

I must admit it's darker than I thought possible. No moon out or anything. "I think I'm going to start calling the ghosts," I say. "Ghosts, come here." My own voice projects louder than I intend.

"Stop, are you crazy?"

"I want to see a ghost."

"Don't. Call. Them," she whispers forcing each word through her teeth.

"If you want, I can hold your hand." Or touch her breasts again.

"You'd like that too much."

I wonder if anybody's ever had sex in the cemetery and realize I'm a horrible person for wondering such a thought. Even though it's still in the middle of a Michigan winter with snow blanketing the ground, Carmen is wearing a skirt, which makes me pay even more attention to her amazing legs.

"You're staring at me, you creep," she says.

"You have the goofiest walk in human history," I say, which is true. "It's like if a robot walked around dressed in a jean skirt."

She punches my arm.

And like that we are back to normal again, if I can even say Carmen and I have a "normal."

Chapter 7

Grandparents are the worst. They're like your parents except more reserved, slower, and *more* out of touch with reality. I'm surprised my grandpa isn't dead yet. I've seen better-looking corpses if we're being perfectly honest.

"The problem with your generation is that you don't pay attention," my grandpa caws—I swear he sounds like a goddamn crow. "You're too busy playing with your phones and obsessing over the newest technology."

Picture a stereotypical old person. They all caw the exact same way with the whole "back-in-my-day-my-parents-made-me-walk-barefoot-in-three-feet-of-snow-and-I-got-hypothermia" bullshit. Their parents didn't love them, so now they take all of their misery out on younger generations because if they're not going to be happy nobody is allowed to be. Gramps is the type that goes to church, votes only republican, dislikes anything not white because he's a racist, and frowns upon "fags prancing around." (His words, not mine.)

His latest rant: unprovoked. All I did was take out my flip phone and glance at it for a split second, praying for a call from anybody to save me from the monthly ritual of Dinner at Gramps.

Gramps can't wrap his head around the fact that I have a cellular unit and I don't need to use a landline to call somebody.

I've paid attention in American History, and I know that his generation has taken part in two wars, they've barely treated Black people like human beings, and they've successfully shut down gay marriage.

It's too cold for his biggest obsession: his yard. He'll meticulously pick every acorn out of it. I used to mow every week for him in the summers as a kid, and he'd give me $20 which seemed like a mini fortune at the time. We'd drink ginger ales on the porch. Now, I only drink ginger ale when I'm sick.

"Are you going to answer me, son?"

Sometimes I just wish he would croak. When he's on life-support, I'm going to unplug it and tell him the technology is "not necessary."

"You didn't ask a question," I say.

"Why is your generation so disrespectful?"

"We're not. We're the most tolerant generation there is. Our school recently started the Gay/Straight Alliance, and many students support gay rights." I decide to poke the crow.

Gramps' face is red, and I can see the muscles in his neck convulsing.

"That's just not *natural*," Gramps caws.

"Neither was segregation, WWII, or Vietnam."

"God made Adam and Eve, not—"

I zone out. I've heard the same goddamn story over two thousand times. Then there was a talking animal in the garden. The whole apple in the garden thing was kind of evil if you ask me. God put the apple there *knowing* full-well they'd eat it. All Satan was doing was saying, "Hey, maybe this God Guy isn't all that great if you think about it? He's asking you not to eat from the tree of *knowledge*, meaning He wants to keep you ignorant and stupid?" Now God put a generational guilt trip on us to be passed down throughout all humanity.

We're supposed to feel guilty for simply being alive even though none of us chose to be.

Legally, you can't even be charged for the crimes of your grandfather and father in the United States. I wish God had the same courtesy.

I'm kind of an atheist if you want to know the truth.

There aren't any interesting characters in the Bible. It's just a bunch of stories, not even *good* stories. The Bible lacks focus and picking over 20 narrators maybe wasn't the best choice, stylistically, for clarity, cohesiveness, or proving an "all knowing" creator exists. Not to mention anytime people didn't do exactly what God wanted them to do, he murdered them. Flooded the Earth. He was jealous and all-around kind of childish.

The book of Job is the worst. The guy's an asshole the way I see it. He loves God so much, and then Satan and God start *betting* on how loyal he is to God, as if it's just some card game or something. Talk about God being a douchebag. Well, Job says he loves God and all that and Satan comes down and kills Job's entire family. The guy doesn't even blink. He just says God is good and boasts about how much he loves God. It's not until Satan gives Job sores and herpes or something like that the man actually starts to question his creator. My point is if Job was *actually* a good guy, he would have been cursing God when he let Satan kill his entire family.

"Are you even listening to me?" Gramps asks.

"I've heard the story before."

I can't wait until I'm 18 and on my own. I'll only visit him on Christmas, Easter, and Thanksgiving. Of course, I'm flexible and willing to make one exception: I'll visit him for his funeral.

On the drive back, Dad gives it to me.

My dad is one of those part-time Christians, meaning he doesn't feel like he needs to go to church to get through the pearly gates, but he does think that a person can only get in if they believe in the God who decided the only way to save humanity was by killing his kid.

"You need to have more patience," Pops explains. He works in a bank and deals with customer complaints all day. He always tells me I need to have more patience.

"He's been through a lot with grandma," Pops adds.

"That was quite a few years ago." Considering I'm 16, and I was about six when she left, I don't even remember any of it.

"Your grandpa comes from a different generation."

After a brief pause, my dad adds, "You have to be conscientious of the age gap."

I *hate* when my dad tries to use big words. He thinks because he uses a big word I have no clue what he means, and I'm unaware of the invention of the dictionary.

"His generation is the least tolerant." The Silent Generation. Which is true. The only thing noteworthy they did was had a bunch of kids, my dad's generation: the Baby Boomers.

"He's been through a lot with grandma and all," he repeats, trying to appeal to ethos, the emotional response.

"Dad would you ever kill me?"

"What?" he looks at me like I've been smoking pot.

"I was just wondering. Say, if you had to for the *greater good of the Earth*."

"I couldn't do it. Never," Pops says.

See what I'm talking about? Simply idiotic.

"Can I drive?" I ask.

"No."

It's a response Pops is used to giving. Nothing better disrupt the routine. Despite the fact I have a driver's license, he never lets me drive his car.

Gramps, for all his flaws, at least trusted me to drive his car since I was 14 and took me to driver's training. In fact, he trained me with most of my driving. Pops would be too critical about every goddamn thing. Apparently, I didn't break as quick as he liked, or I wouldn't turn how he wanted.

Gramps first words of advice were, "Don't let anybody give you shit. There's a lot of bad drivers on the road."

One time driving by Pere Marquette on a road that goes by the beach and Lake Michigan this guy behind me rode my ass. I got a little scared.

"Maybe I should just pull off?"

"No," Gramps said.

We kept driving like this. Finally, when we came to a stop sign, Gramps said, "Break now. Hard."

"What?"

"Break hard. Now."

I did.

The guy behind me hit me.

Gramps stormed out of the car and started yelling at the guy. "You're at fault. You just rear-ended us. You're going to get a ticket."

The guy ended up speeding off.

"Don't we have to wait for the cops?"

"Just go. This old thing already has dents. But I guarantee you, he'll never do that again."

I sit silently for the rest of the twenty-minute drive home, watching trees pass until we're in our suburb of Muskegon, Michigan. The same town my dad grew up in and lived his whole life. The same town he'll die in.

Later, I catch Pops petting, Winona, our gray tabby cat. "You'll never leave us," he baby-talks, stroking under her chin as she tils her head up, eyes closed. Sometimes she resembles a dragon.

She used to be a stray. One day he heard meowing in the back yard and she appeared, skin and bones. Her front teeth were missing, and at first, we thought her tail had been hacked off, but the vet informed us it was because she's a tabby cat, and she naturally has a shorter tail.

My dad brought her food and blankets.

Despite my dad's heroic efforts, she took off after his rescue for about three or four months. It was a very depressing time for my old man. I could only imagine how he would have been when mom left—listless, devoid of purpose, sitting there with his whiskey at night, rarely saying much—but, alas, my memory fails to recount anything about mom leaving, and I don't think I got that it was a permanent fixture in our living situation at the time.

"I just can't imagine how she's making it out there in the world," he said, staring out the window.

The truth is before us she survived four years—according to the vet estimate. Meaning she's known not having us more than she's known having us.

She eventually came back, stick-skinny and frail.

And this is the story of how Winona became a house cat. My dad refuses to let her outside anymore because he thinks she'll just run off. Regardless, she's escaped captivity three times.

I'm standing in the hallway, watching my dad; he's unaware of my presence or doesn't care at this point.

"You are loved," he says. "You my girl and it will never change." He says this softer, barely audible. Winona's purrs hum loudly across the room, louder than my dad's voice. One of the rare moments she's complacent in his arms instead of squirming or running away.

Like I said, when Pops decided to domesticate her, he took her to the vet. Got her checked for ticks, fleas, and made the vets run a bunch of tests. Updated her on shots. We found out she was spayed, meaning at one point in time she belonged to somebody else, but she either left because she wanted to—whether to be free or due to abuse—or they abandoned her.

Ironically, my dad never allowed *me* to have a pet, even when I would repeatedly ask as a child—and the furthest he allowed was fish, but they died repeatedly. Eventually naming them seemed redundant, and the worst part: they were boring. But because of a whim, he decided to foster the stray cat of the neighborhood, and we now have Winona.

Chapter 8

Fourth hour is pre-calc. I think I've developed some type of selective ADD over the course of my educational career. If something is not interesting, I tune out. This includes most math and science classes. Thankfully, once this year is over, I will have completed the two required years of math and science.

Mr. Lysinger stands in front of the room, droning on in his monotone voice about the equation on the board. I swear there are subatomic particles in his voice that could put anybody to sleep.

"As you can see here …"

I stare ahead at the board. I can't stand how Mr. Gensen called me into his office. I wasn't mad about it then, but I am kind of fuming now, which is kind of weird considering it happened last week.

Mr. Lysinger stopped talking, and I realize my favorite part of the class is about to take place. His aid, Mr. Laurel, is going to go over the homework. Unlike Lysinger's monotone voice, Laurel has a Boston accent.

"Which one would you like me to go over first?" he asks.

"How about four?" Aaron, who sits in the front of the room, requests.

"Awight, let's go over fawr."

After he does, I request the next one. "How about number fourteen?"

"Fawteen?"

"Yes."

Aaron raises his hand, "Number 24."

"Twenty fawr."

I suppress my laughter to the best of my ability. Mr. Laurel is the much-needed comical relief.

Next, I raise my hand, "How about 44?"

"Fawty fawr?" Laurel repeats.

The whole class bursts out laughing at this point.

"Enough," Mr. Lysinger says from his desk. "Forty-four wasn't even assigned."

Chapter 9

In government class we're going to have an election. All of us got to choose which party to be in: Democratic or Republican. At the beginning of the semester, we had to take a survey that asked questions such as, "How do you feel about a person's right to view pornography in the privacy of their own home?"

Carmen was over-curious what answer I put for this question.

I was damn near in the middle when it came to political parties on his stupid questionnaire. I think as long as people aren't hurting anybody, they should be allowed to do what they want. And to be perfectly honest, it's not really a topic that interests me all too much. It's just a bunch of idiots going on and on about what they think.

Our teacher, Mr. Hopper, believes in doing push-ups when kids behave inappropriately, especially when the male students talk back. I've had to do the most push-ups out of anybody in class. At the beginning of the year, we had to write a flashcard with our name on it, where we thought we'd be in ten years, and a "thought to ponder."

For my thought to ponder I wrote, "I wonder if there is handicap parking in the Special Olympics."

When he read it, he said, "You should do 10 push-ups for karma, Mr. McCarthy."

For where I put where I'd be in ten years, I wrote, "the circus." I would perform tricks or walk on the tightrope, and I've always wanted to pet a tiger. I know in the long run it wouldn't work out and while everybody is sleeping, I would set all the animals free.

"I want each of you to join either the Republican Party or the Democratic Party based on the questionnaire you took at the beginning of the semester," Mr. Hopper instructs.

"You can break off and create separate parties if you wish," he reminds us.

"Has that ever worked?" somebody asks from the front of the class.

"One year, Mitch Alan's Independent Party won," he says. "As a reminder, the party who wins the election wins extra credit."

I landed slightly on the Republican Party, so opted to join their squad.

Riley quickly turns around in her seat to face me. "What happened with you and Carmen?"

"I don't know what you're talking about."

"McCarthy, what happened?"

"Nothing."

She turns her head back, and I almost want to think I imagined this moment, a split in reality, but I know I didn't.

So, Carmen doesn't tell everybody everything? I wondered about this—*who* and *what* did she tell others about us?

We have all of our desks rammed together like one giant mob.

Then it begins.

"So ... abortion," Andrew Raborn reads. We decided he would be our spokesperson, or rather the rest of the group decided as I couldn't care less. "Are we for it or against it?"

"Against," almost everybody mumbles at once.

Here's the thing: I personally don't want my baby to be aborted and would encourage a girl to not give up my kid, but who am I to tell anybody else what they do if they decide to knock out a microscopic spec of could-be life before it knows what's going on?

"It's my body, so it should be my right to choose," Riley says. She clearly belongs to the Democratic Party and will argue every single issue.

A few members let out an audible sigh.

The debate continues. Next on the docket: gay marriage. Universally the group goes against this one.

"But I have a gay friend," Riley says. "You're telling me he could never get married?"

"Marriage is between a man and woman," Ben Benson, this curly-haired kid with brown eyes who looks like a stoner but has never touched a drop of alcohol or pot in his life, says.

"That's not fair," Riley says.

"What's next, we're going to allow a person to marry a goat?" Benson asks.

A few members laugh.

Really, the problem with either party is they're so set on their goddamn beliefs no matter what. I don't get how they arrived at the bold conclusions about what they stand for on issues. Both accuse the other of being Nazis. But either way you go about it, you have extreme Republicans who hate minorities, and claim to want less government but enforce laws based on an invisible Sky Man. Or you have extreme Democrats who want communism—for us to all get Cs in class no matter how hard we work—and need Big Brother to tie their shoelaces.

If I'm going to be honest, I'm more of an anarchist than anything. We should eliminate all government.

"Why are you even in the group if you disagree with every issue?" Raborn asks Riley. "Are you sure you're in the right group?"

Across the room, Rylan says, "I'm breaking up and forming my own party."

About a third of the Democrat group breaks off.

"Congratulations Democrats, you just lost the election," Mr. Hopper says loud enough where I can hear him but not the entire class.

Chapter 10

Carmen's friend Alexis' older brother's friend—who happens to be 21—was *supposed* to buy us booze. When I say "us" I am referring to an undisclosed number of my peers. Alcohol and possible debauchery bring out many people from various groups.

Unfortunately, he backed out at the last minute leaving us to fend for ourselves.

Four of us are driving in the car, ready to set up tonight's festivities. The first stop: R&B Liquor Store. The store sits on the heights side across town but within view of the highway.

A commonly known fact among my peers: they sell to minors.

"There's nothing like supporting a family-owned business in our neighborhood," Luke Hanson says from the back seat. Carmen drives her hand-me-down Buick from her dad. I ride shottie while Luke and Josh sit in the back seat. I was shocked when Carmen ordered Luke to sit in the back.

"So we just walk in, pay for it, and leave?" I'm skeptical of this plan. Perhaps an officer of the law is hiding behind the counter and will jump out, arrest us, and thwart our Friday night fun.

"That's what everybody says," Josh says.

"They do it all the time," Luke says, nonchalantly, trying to appear cool.

"Have you done it before?" I ask.

"No." Luke looks down. "I mean I know people who have."

Our car gets closer to the store as we cross the highway.

"I don't think we should all go in," Carmen says.

"Why not?" Josh asks.

"It might be too much for them. Only one of us should go."

I know who she'll elect before it even comes out of her mouth. "McCarthy should do it," Carmen volunteers me.

"Why not Luke? He seems to have more insider knowledge than me."

"Are you scared or something?" Luke sneers.

"I'll do it."

I take a deep breath as I exit the car door, look back, knowing that this could end poorly. But my feet keep walking, the same way they kept walking up to Carmen's locker the first time in September, regardless of what my brain was telling me.

I open the door. There's an old Middle Eastern man standing behind the counter. He looks at me indifferently. I go over to the beer and grab a case of 30 beers. I don't bother scanning too many. We need as much beer as we possibly can get and thirty sounds like a lot. The box is heavy, pulling my arm out of its socket as I carry it to the counter.

"Will that be all?" the old man asks.

I notice a cigarillo, watermelon flavor and say, "I'll take one of those as well."

"That'll be $20.15." I hand him a 20 and fish for change in my pocket, unsure if I even have any.

"Don't worry about the change," he says.

I pocket the cigarillo and haul the case of beer out to the car. I fight every instinct I have not to run out of the store as I march as quickly as I can to the car.

"Open up the trunk," I yell.

Carmen follows suit, and I put the case in.

"Phase one of our plan is complete," Carmen says.

"There's more than one phase?"

Chapter 11

Phase two of the plan involves more people at Alexis' house. To ensure law enforcement efforts are not wasted and taxpayer dollars are not squandered, we have devised a plan.

The idea is relatively simple: We are cramming at least ten people into each vehicle in order not to draw attention to the fact that numerous people will be in Alexis' house—whose parents happen to be out of town this weekend.

"Everybody better bring their own booze," I say. "Thirty beers will not provide beer for everyone. I call dibs on at least five of them."

I'm unsure of the number of beers needed to achieve inebriation. I'm more accustomed to drinking vodka and other stuff because it's easier to carry around and less bulky. Not to mention having a full liquor cabinet at my disposal.

"They will," Carmen says, reassuringly.

"Who all did you invite?"

"Typical McCarthy behavior. I could tell you I have one million dollars in my hand and want to spend it with you and you'd want to know who is else is coming with."

"Not true."

"You're judgmental."

"Not as picky as some people."

"But you judge."

I pause for emphasis. "I judge you because you're about the most annoying person on the face of the entire planet."

Carmen smirks and sticks out her tongue. I wish my tongue was touching hers and they were dancing around in our mouths.

I walk away for a second. Carmen follows me. "Can I help you?" I ask. I turn away.

"Stop it. You know I hate when you do that."

Three cars prove to be enough, and we have over thirty people in one house with ample amounts of booze. Meanwhile, our cars are in a church parking lot that officers seldom frequent—we know this because many transactions go down in the parking lot during non-church hours that I will not go into detail about.

People arrive, making me question Carmen's popularity and outreaching abilities at Lakewood High School.

More people arrive than I imagine.

Luke Hanson struts around. My intestines clench, and I realize my fists are clenched as well. I watch as he walks towards Carmen who is commiserating with a group of our peers, talking and laughing.

I gulp down another beer, the bitter taste hitting my taste buds. While tolerable, not desirable. I go to the bathroom.

A complexity I've noticed since consuming alcohol. They say when you're super hydrated you piss clear, but alcohol is supposed to dehydrate the hell out of you. How come every time I'm drunk, I piss clear?

I approach the group Carmen's with.

"This one time I got pulled over by the cops," Luke says. "I had like three or four shots. The officer asked if I had been drinking and I said, *Well, I'm not drunk*. The officer just stood there and didn't know what to say, so he didn't even breathalyze me or make me walk the line."

Everybody laughs despite it being a friggen awful unfunny story.

"That sounds very plausible," I say.

He glares at me.

"It's true. It happened."

I've heard his stories.

"It doesn't mask the undeniable smell of bullshit when I hear you tell it." My teeth clench.

Carmen puts her hand on my arm.

Luke stares at me with the intensity of someone who wants to fight.

"Are you still bothering Carmen and taking all your frustration out on her? Or did you finally leave her alone and let her breathe?"

What has she told him?

I walk away. Carmen follows.

When we're away from the group, I ask, "What did you tell him?" We sit side by side.

Carmen looks at me. She rests her head on my shoulder.

I push her away.

"What did you tell him?"

"I was upset at the time and I didn't mean anything by—"

"You want everyone to make fun of me and look down at me."

There's a long silence. Sometimes I find her so irresistible; other times I wish I never met her.

"I'm not a trophy you know..." She says this quietly, almost defeated.

No, she's not. She's like this dream you've had, something you've been chasing, not only a feeling but an endgame you didn't even know you wanted—when you're together it's like you're high and drunk even though you didn't do either. And you want that feeling all the time, but just when you get close to her, she pulls away.

"You're more like a hemorrhoid. Literally a pain in the ass."

More people arrive in another crammed vehicle. Carmen looks oddly worried.

"There's way too many people here," Carmen says.

She is shushed by Alexis when she brings up her concern.

I realize how close Carmen is standing to me, leaning up next to me on the table. Definitely within my personal bubble.

"Are you guys like—" Alexis makes a together motion with her fingers when looking at Carmen and me.

"Eww, definitely not," I say.

Carmen punches me in the arm. I haven't noticed her punch any other guys in the arm. I wonder if she sometimes does, but I'd like to think of this as a special sign of affection she only shares with me. I debate asking her.

After being at the house for a couple of hours, I realize my level of inebriation is particularly high—my body functions aren't as fluent, while I am not slurring or stumbling, I am impaired.

There is a knock on the door.

Alexis peeks out. "Shit, it's the cops," she says.

Everybody starts running. Which in all honesty probably is not the best possible solution. Instead, we should have cut the music and hid. Pretended nobody was home.

"This was such a *great* idea," I say to Carmen before we take off.

"I'll make it up to you," she promises. "And I'll make up for being an ass earlier."

When I get home my dad is asleep on the sofa, as he sometimes is on a Friday night. A bottle of whiskey by him. I can faintly smell it as I step into the room, put the glass into the sink, and make my way into bed.

Winona looks at me and meows. She follows me up the stairs to my room.

The saddest part about my dad's Winona obsession is the painful fact she doesn't care for him. Every time he picks her up, she squirms, attempting to get away. When he pets her, she sometimes tolerates it but only on the you're-the-one-that's-feeding-me-so-I-have-to-like-you level. I've never witnessed her going out of her way to sit by him, and her sleeping spot remains far from his bed.

His desperation is almost embarrassing, but I'm the only witness present.

Winona comes up to me regularly. She needs her cuddles otherwise she gets grumpy. She sits on me, and I pet her behind her ears how she likes it. I rub my nose against hers and she doesn't pull away. Eskimo kisses. She purrs loudly, a roar that vibrates my entire being.

"You're a good girl. You're safe. I love you."

She continues to purr as I massage her head with my hands in circular motions, under her chin and those soft spots in front of her ears with no hair.

"I'll always love you."

Winona doesn't stay in bed with me because she's a free spirit. She loves cuddling me, but she likes to roam free, to make her own choices, to not just be a product of a society forcing her to be something she isn't.

I admire her will.

Chapter 12

It's a fairly clear night, meaning it's possible to gaze into the vastness of space. It's weird thinking about how it goes on infinitely. It makes me wonder if it just means it's too big for scientists to process, so instead of saying maybe someday it will be this calculated entity—literally everything—they say "infinite" so commonplace people bad at science like myself don't ask questions and accept this as a unanimous truth.

Carmen agreed to accompany me tonight, a first. It's unusual but I think it's her weird way to make up for the party. We're sitting on my roof, a space I realized can be reached with relative ease once I popped out my screen on my second-story bedroom window. Pops showed me how to do it as a kid, so I'd have a fire escape; I don't think he knew I'd use to sit on the roof when I felt like it.

"What did you tell Luke?" I ask, something that's been bothering me.

"Not much. He's a friend. I just didn't know how to handle it all ..."

"A friend?"

"I've talked to him since freshman year. Believe me, if something would have happened between Luke and I, it would have by now."

I let this sink in. We stare up into the night sky. I still don't like the idea she'd tell someone else stuff when I don't even *know* the whole story.

"You realize when we're staring out into space we're really looking back in time," I say.

She doesn't say anything.

"Because it takes so long for light to travel to us, that star right there could have already burnt out but we don't know because the light from it takes thirty years to reach us."

"Are you high?"

"Completely sober. It's a trippy thought. And if aliens had a telescope and saw us, they're seeing us as we were many years ago. They might see us sitting here looking up in thirty years. Or they might see dinosaurs and are unaware there's even human life on Earth."

"You don't believe in aliens."

"I don't believe in much."

Humanity will disappoint you. Life will get better in the future. One day we won't need to go to the liquor store we know sells to minors. One day Carmen and I will live our own separate lives. Will we still talk? We'll have jobs and I don't know what else …

"Why do you have to cheat in science then?"

"This is Astronomy. I never cheated in Astronomy. I suck at labs and math, people actually copied *me* in Astronomy. Or, as I would say, I *loaned them answers*."

She snorts.

We stare into the void. Specks of stars highlight the sky, as big if not bigger than our sun, yet they seem so far away.

"Which star is that?" Carmen asks. The brightest star in the sky.

"Sirius, also known as the Dog Star," I say. "In Greek, it means glowing. It was mentioned back in 150 AD. It's 8.6 light-years away. It's 20 times brighter than the sun."

"What about that one?" Carmen asks, pointing to a moving blinking object.

"That's a plane."

"Oh, I knew that."

"It's cute you're trying at least. We might make a little astronomer out of you yet."

She elbows my ribcage.

"Maybe it's a UFO."

"It's most definitely a plane."

And I wonder if somebody will watch us in the future, Carmen and me, on my roof. At first, the stars and space made me feel so small. Earth is nothing but a mere speck, but in the eternity of space, all of us are only a brief insignificant microscopic speck. Sometimes I try to remember this. The first time I mustered up the courage to talk to Carmen, I thought about this. Even if I fail, nobody notices. It means nothing in the scheme of the universe.

"It's weird all the stars were here centuries before we were born, but maybe some of them died out already," I say.

And I feel like our star burnt out long before I even knew it existed.

Chapter 13

Women & Minorities is known as a slack class. Like many of my peers, I sprinkle a few "slack classes"—classes where the teacher notoriously under assigns homework or assigns none at all—into my schedule each semester.

The first day each of us had to share from our seats why we took the class.

I said, "I took this class because I heard it's a slack class."

This generated laughter.

The teacher, Mr. Gardner—who had seemed laid back up to this point—didn't even smile. He glared at me and said, "We can change that."

My friend, Alex, who sat next to me whispered, "Maybe you shouldn't have said that."

I've been told this many times after I say something by teachers, parents, and even fellow peers I barely know. It has yet to deter me.

Afterwards, a stoner, Jerry, was called on. He said, "I took this class because I heard there was going to be lots of homework."

We went into a lot of back-story. To be honest, we haven't exactly done all that much, but I'm not complaining about ending the day on my easiest hour. A blonde ditz a grade older than me dropped the class after a few days.

"What's a minority?" she asked us. "Isn't it a branch of government?"

We explained it to her.

"I thought it was a branch of government," she repeated.

I *wish* I was making this up. While we all live very sheltered lives surrounded by kids in a community that can do no wrong—with, yes, mostly white kids; I said it—all of us knew what a minority was. At least we're aware diversity exists. Or can exist. Recently, our school's gotten more diverse with School of Choice.

"I want us to talk about all different groups and their stereotypes," Mr. Gardner says. He writes the word, *Asians*, on the whiteboard.

Nobody speaks.

"Come on," Mr. Gardner says. "I'm not trying to get anybody in trouble here. We're going to look at these things."

"Short," somebody says.

"Good. Short." He writes the word on the board.

"Can't drive," I say.

Laughter erupts.

He pauses for a second and writes it on the board.

"Their names sound how when you drop silverware," JaShaun, one of the three African Americans in the class, says. The class has a few more girls in it than guys.

Next, we do African American stereotypes.

The room goes completely silent.

"Is it even Black people or African Americans?" somebody asks.

Mr. Gardner turns to the three students, all sitting together, and asks, "What do you guys think? Is the term African Americans better or Black people?"

"Black people," the one girl, Denise, says. "I've never been to Africa, so I think it's weird being referred to a place I've never been to."

"Lazy," JaShaun says, adding a word to the board.

"In a gang," somebody says.

We continue adding more words to the board.

Next, Mr. Gardner writes "Caucasians" on the board.

"That word's always puzzled me," a red-headed senior, Aurora, says. "There's nowhere on the globe called Caucasia."

"What are some words you'd use to describe white people?" Mr. Gardner says to the three Black students in the room.

"You guys are too curious. You play with fire and all that," JaShaun says. "You don't see any of us chasing tornados or playing with fire."

This generates quite a bit of laughter from the room, including me.

"Can't jump," I yell.

More laughter erupts.

"Can't jump," Mr. Gardner repeats. "The purpose of all of this is to recognize these harmful descriptions and classifications of those around you. Oftentimes, they're not true, but they're used in a derogatory manner to gain a sense of control."

Chapter 14

I'm in first hour Writing in Print with Mr. Cannon. He's decent enough and looks the part of a weathered journalist with a thick gray beard, a strained face with dark knowing eyes, and journalism experience. And I wouldn't be surprised if he keeps a bottle of scotch in one of his desk drawers.

We have articles due every two weeks to give us time to conduct interviews, write the articles, and receive edits from Mr. Cannon.

It's a small class and each of us has our own niches.

Mr. Cannon labels my writing as rants. He says they can be funny, which is good, and makes people want to read them. But, as he always reminds me, I need to conduct more interviews, do more research, and try to appeal to a wider audience.

Marcie Erins covers all of the fluff pieces. She's written on pageants in the past, interviewed the cheerleading squad, and has written numerous articles on the importance of school spirit. She's the type of person best in small five-minute doses, especially in the morning.

Jeanna Smith is super conservative, goes to church every Sunday. She'll cover anything related to volunteering or people trying to appear like they are a good person. She's the type of person who would start crying if you said the word "penis."

Mark Burley strictly covers sports, whether it's interviews with the coaches and players or the direct results of the game. He'll break it all down, play by play, and knows more about sports than any reasonable human should.

Blane Colly is the closest we have to someone who covers "news." Lakewood isn't exactly the hot spot of murders, robberies, and other crimes. But good old Blane with his glasses and straight-forward thinking covers the "news" the best he can.

Last and least, there's Carl Denton. He used to live here but moved to Texas for ten years. He'll constantly remind us how everything is bigger in Texas. Unfortunately, brainpower must not be one of these commodities. I'll sometimes smoke with him, but the kid's kind of a mooch. Always asking for lunch money or money to buy pot. The worst part: he has no noticeable talents in the writing department. Or any other talents for that matter whatsoever. He took the class just to fill his schedule. He told me so. He has yet to find a niche. One time he thought he could cover sports, but he missed all of the key parts. At the end of the game, he couldn't tell you any of the player's names or even the score of the game.

"Today, we're going to talk about something important all of you will run into if you attempt a career as a budding journalist," Mr. Cannon says.

He gets out his red marker to write on the whiteboard, which indicates the matter is of importance.

"All of you will run into *bullshit*," he writes the word on the board, like a textbook term. "Can anybody define *bullshit?*"

Nobody says anything. Even the most-hardened wanna-be journalist knows this isn't in any of our textbooks.

"Mr. McCarthy, can you define *bullshit?*"

"Why did you call on me?"

The class laughs.

"We all know why," Carl Denton jokes. A rare moment of clever contribution from his mouth.

"All joking aside, how would you define the term, Mr. McCarthy?" Mr. Cannon looks at me.

"It's when somebody isn't being truthful, and it's clear the second they open their mouth."

"Very good. Exactly. As a journalist you will need to have a clear working bullshit detector. People will lie right to your face, and it's up to you to look into what they say. Talk to others. Find supporting evidence, through documents, court records, and medical records."

I write down the word *bullshit* in my notebook.

"Good to see you taking notes Mr. McCarthy, although I suspect you won't have to for this one."

The class laughs, and I'm the dunce.

"You start to lose respect for people the first time a politician lies to your face," Mr. Cannon continues. "It's important to be aware that what somebody says isn't always true. This is why it's so important to find all the information. Interview many people."

Luckily, for me, I have a very good sense of when somebody is telling the truth or if they're just giving you the run around. In fact, I've already run into this a few times while working for the school paper. Certain things the administrators skirt around, especially any question regarding politics in sports.

Mr. Cannon shifts gears. "I want somebody to write an article for the Snow Coming Dance. I know it's a ways off, but I still want it covered in the next paper."

Dances are stupid. People who dance look ridiculous, moving around like mentally deranged primates. It's a waste of energy. But for some reason, the ladies tend to like it. As a result, I have found myself at a few different ones. To say the least, it's not something I found enjoyable, even while intoxicated.

"Part of the student paper is to inform your classmates about upcoming events. In this case, this is a piece to hype it up. I give you many liberties you will not have when you are writing for a newspaper."

Instead of having our main focus on our Homecoming, Lakewood High School created a dance called Snow Coming. I know, I know, it's trying to be clever when it isn't, and it doesn't make sense considering it's in April. You see, our football team is about the worst football team in the entire state. We're lucky if we win a single game the entire season. Naturally, for Homecoming you're supposed to pick a team you know you'll whip the crap out of. The problem is no team is a *guaranteed* win with our football program and often the administration chooses wrong.

Last homecoming our football team didn't even play much of a game. We played a school we were told by all the football players we had a chance of beating. We were down 49-0 by halftime and it started raining. We proposed numerous solutions. We could substitute the soccer team for the football team? Or the band? Or maybe even the cheerleaders?

We started cheering for the other team, despite receiving dirty looks from all of the parents.

Most of us left by half time.

The flyers will be up around school in a month or so. Months of planning go into Snow Coming each year. They'll announce a Snow Coming King and a Snow Coming Queen. They still do all the homecoming stuff and have a king and queen for that, but to be honest all of the hype is about the Snow Coming Dance. I even grace the dance with my presence each year.

"As much as you know how much I'm not a fan of fluff pieces, I do want this article to be more of a *fluff* piece as it's been a tradition at Lakewood High for the past twenty years."

Fluff pieces are basically articles written like you'd find in a gossip magazine.

"Any volunteers?" Mr. Cannon asks.

I look down.

Marcie raises her hand. "I'll do it."

"You already have two pieces," Mr. Cannon says. "I can't ask you to take on a third. I want somebody to take a chance here. Find new angles and people to interview."

I sink further into my seat, hoping for the love of every deity out there he doesn't choose me.

"Mr. McCarthy, how about you?"

"I don't feel like I'd be the best candidate for such an endeavor."

He stares at me.

"I mean, I don't know if I could adequately cover the piece in time."

He still looks at me, silent.

"You weren't really asking, were you?"

"No, I wasn't. I am assigning it to you. Workplace advice in future newsrooms; when your editor asks if you will cover something, you do it."

People always do that. Ask questions that are not really questions. We get told so much about what will be expected of us in the "adult world" and how we have it easy here, but I don't think they understand. For one thing, at least then I'll be *paid* for writing about something I couldn't care less about. For another, I'm not going to be dragged through Physics or Pre-Calc after.

"I can't believe you used a swear word as like a term," Jeanna Smith says. Like I said before, if you told her where babies came from, she'd probably lose her mind.

"Don't worry. This won't be a term on the final exam, and don't bother trying to get me in trouble," Mr. Cannon says. "I've been doing this for over ten years. Do you really think the school will fire me?"

The bell rings.

Chapter 15

Gym class—officially known as Sports Skills—provides a much-needed change of pace. While I'm not crazy about lifting weights or playing sports, it's not so bad. Even when we play floor hockey, the kids who are actually on the hockey team barely try, so we can have an actual game.

I opt out of doing squats like I always do. The whole weight-lifting thing and watching each of my male contemporaries grunt and sweat while lifting heavy weight doesn't appeal to me. Each brags to the other, asserting he is more muscular and stronger.

This kid, Paul, comes up to me as I do curls. "Has anybody ever told you that you have good veins for heroin?"

"No, that would be a first."

Then it's time for our favorite part: hitting the showers. I wonder what sort of pervert had the idea to put all the students in one big room to shower with no dividers. It's kind of strange if you really think about it.

Locker Room Talk commences. While the same people generate it the majority of the time, occasionally someone else chimes in.

"Is Lauren's birthday coming up?" Connor asks Nick.

"Yeah."

"What are you going to do for her birthday?"

"She's going to suck my cock."

"She's going to suck your cock on *her* birthday?"

"Yes."

"Is she still tight?"

"You know it," Nick says. "I'm working on loosening her up."

Chapter 16

We're blessed with the fortunes of having a sub in Pre-Calc.

The substitute fumbles with a piece of paper in his hand.

"Aaron Andrews."

"Here."

"Samantha Bursk."

"Here."

"Norman Klinsky."

"Here."

Before he even finishes reading my name, I say, "Present."

Everybody looks at me like I'm the biggest pain in the ass.

"Today we're going to talk about different kinds of people," the substitute begins. "Aliens visited Earth before and their spaceship will come back in the future."

We exchange 'is-this-guy-serious?' glances with each other.

The last substitute teacher insisted on us teaching the class and sat in a desk while he asked students to explain the lesson.

I swear they'll let anybody walk into Lakewood and teach classes.

"There are red people, green people, and purple people," the substitute teacher continues. His frizzled hair indicates perhaps an overindulgence in LSD when he was younger. We know all of our parents did a crap-ton of drugs in the 70s and 80s, but maybe they shouldn't let the people who did too much teach the students?

"One day the spaceship will return to earth and the people will go into different categories."

While slightly entertaining and thankfully completely un-math related, this is a bit much.

He continues explaining his alien theories to the class. All in all, I've had more entertaining classes, but it beats the usual routine.

I raise my hand, "Can I go to the bathroom?"

The instructor looks puzzled as to why somebody would want to leave his hippy-induced trippy rant about aliens and the vast possibilities of space.

He signs my notebook and continues blabbering as I leave the class.

"The first time the aliens came to the earth ..."

I know it's Mr. Cannon's free hour.

I'm thankful it's Thursday and I have to only make it through today and one more day until freedom.

Each week, before our article is printed, Mr. Cannon goes over our articles with each of us. Sometimes this is in between classes, and he writes us a note. Other times during class. Other times we'll stay after school for a little bit. They're short sessions when he edits—and more importantly (in his opinion)—provides us places where we should cut out what we wrote.

Blane Connelly is in the classroom and grabs his bag when I enter. Before he leaves, he says, "McCarthy, did you hear about the new Apple phone? It's called an iPhone. It's going to change the whole world and put the power of an entire computer into every person's hand."

"That sounds *very* believable," I say. Everyone always has all these crazy ideas for technological advances.

"Dork," I tease jokingly as he brushes past me.

I present my rough draft of my Snow Coming article to Mr. Cannon.

Mr. Cannon reads over my draft. While he generally skims and edits articles for grammar and clarity, he's really scrutinizing this one, and I have the feeling he doesn't trust me.

To understand the Snow Coming Dance, one needs to go back to the origin of it. Lakewood High's rich tradition of the unorthodox dance dates back to 1983, when Holly Hunter, the head cheerleader and leader of the student body, proposed the dance during a planning committee.

There's no secret as to the reason behind the dance. Because our school lacks a respectable football team, Snow Coming is regarded as our replacement for homecoming. Our football has a long history of struggling to win an entire game in one season (sorry, football team, and no offense Mr. Gardner). Due to this and the dampened spirits after the game, it was decided that since we have an all-star hockey team, we should have a dance in the spring when the snow (sometimes) starts to melt.

"I don't know about this part right here, Mr. McCarthy."

He points to the part that reads, *Because our school lacks a respectable football team, Snow Coming is regarded as our replacement for homecoming.*

"What?" It is true. Our school hasn't had a respectable football team ever. Even back in my dad's day—he graduated 30 years before me—the football team sucked.

"Do you think a certain function in our athletic program might find this line offensive?"

"The football team is a joke and should know they are a joke."

"Mr. McCarthy, football players, Mr. Gardner, and others might find this harsh. Not to mention, it is unnecessary to the story."

Mr. Cannon looks up at me. "Maybe cut out the part about the football team entirely?"

"You know it's true. Besides, I wouldn't be a true journalist if I didn't expose the truth."

"Remember what I said about general public knowledge?"

"Not to include it?"

"Saying the football team sucks is like saying the earth is round."

"I'll cut it," I say, begrudgingly. Even though I want to include it. He's always making us cut stuff from our stories; in the end, it's better off to listen to what he has to say. I've tried him in the past, but since he's an adult, he thinks he always knows better. Then again, I mean he had some journalism experience, so he probably has better judgment than most other adults. Ultimately, he leaves some choices up to us, but he is the final judge.

"I think it'll strengthen your story. It's a good piece."

This means I have until Wednesday (or sometime early Thursday) to make all necessary changes. The paper comes out on Fridays.

By the end of Friday, you will either have people yelling at you down the hallways, giving you some type of praise, or giving you strange looks. I've had all three happen to me throughout my career for *The Lakewood Bi-Weekly*. Sometimes even during the same *day*.

"Good work. Maybe I'll make a journalist of you one day."

Chapter 17

Carl Denton tags along, as he sometimes does, for an after-school drug deal.

"I'll be there in ten minutes," Stan Ellis—perhaps the finest drug dealer Lakewood High has ever seen—says when I called him. In typical stoner mannerism, this would translate to, "I'll be there in half an hour if not later." But with Ellis, he literally means ten minutes.

"Can I borrow $20?" Denton asks me. Like I said before, the kid is a complete mooch. I hand him $20, knowing the chances of me recovering this money is about the same as him not mentioning the time he lived in Texas several times in the next half hour.

"I can't believe Dianna Watson's rack," he says. "I thought everything was bigger in Texas, but if you grow them like that up here ..."

"We have some decent looking girls around here-"

"I've noticed. Big racks and nice asses."

Great wholesome conversation.

"You guys don't have the bongs we had in Texas. I smoked out of the biggest bong I've ever seen ..."

He continues telling me a story as we wait in the car. Parked behind the Cinema Carousel, the only movie theater in town. I zone out. The thing about someone like Denton is I know everything he's saying is complete bullshit. My detector went off the first day of school when he opened his mouth. He overcompensates for being 5' 4" by telling these grand stories of his craziness, but I don't think he's fooling anybody. He's the type of kid that could clear out a lunch table in a matter of minutes. As a result, his transition back to Lakewood High has been anything but easy for him, and I don't think he has any real friends.

"What can I get you?" Stan Ellis pulls up. His car idles parallel to mine facing opposite directions. It's rumored you can call him anywhere in Muskegon and he'll show up (most of the time stoned) in ten minutes. Today, he showed up in five minutes in the desolate parking lot.

His eyes are red and the smell of pot wafts from his car.

"Let me see what you got," Denton says.

Stan looks at him, wearily.

"I want to see thirty dollars and forty."

Stan hands us two bags. At the speed reserved for a senior citizen, Carl looks at the bags.

"Can I see a $20 bag?" Carl asks.

"Dude, you ask too much." Ellis looks at him like he wants to slap him across the face.

"I'll take a dime," I say. The smallest unit of measure: $10 worth. I pride myself on being a simple man when it comes to drug transactions.

Stan hands me the dime as I extend $10 out of the window. Carl shifts the bags between his hands. For a second, I wonder if he's planning to snatch one.

He hands the bags back to me, and I hand them back to Ellis. Carl debates for an unreasonable amount of time considering the circumstances.

"I'll take $40."

It's rumored you can measure Ellis' weed and it will be spot on. He has his shit down to a science. One time last year, he sold a bunch of pot at Lake Harbor in the parking lot. Cars lined up, filling the whole parking lot.

As Carl hands me $40, I hand it to Ellis. He takes it and tosses the bag through the car. "Have a good one fellas. You know who to get in touch with if you need anything else."

Chapter 18

We vote anonymously in our "election" in government class. Voting is mandatory. Mr. Hopper reminds us, "Voting is a necessary part of the democratic process in America."

If you want to look at too much of our history, "discovering" land where people already lived, purposely exposing them to diseases, pushing them out, and committing genocide, America can't always argue we're on the side of virtue.

Everybody always points out the whole World War II thing, but honestly, would America have intervened if Japan had not bombed the shit out of Pearl Harbor?

Questionable.

And sure, it's not the same as killing millions of Jews, but America did drop the only nuke ever used in warfare, wiping out hundreds of thousands of civilians. Everybody remembers the first part but develops amnesia when the latter is mentioned.

"If you get anything out of this class, please take this with you," Mr. Hopper says. He doesn't even sound dramatic when he says this. Maybe it's a requirement by the state to say it. "Always vote. When you turn eighteen, you get that right. Exercise it. You get to choose who's in power."

I resist snorting but make a noise.

"Mr. McCarthy, do you have something to add?" Mr. Hopper asks.

"I didn't say anything."

"You were snickering, sir. Please enlighten the class."

Everybody acts like you *need* to choose somebody. The best choice in a bad multiple-choice questionnaire where all of the answers suck. Instead, I opt out of the question and pretend it's like the SAT. Wrong answers hurt your score. Guessing isn't always the best option.

"You don't want to hear it."

"Please, I want to know what's so funny about voting."

Sometimes people don't want to know. I tried practicing civility and not expressing my opinion about the beloved sacred "democratic process."

The whole class looks back at me.

"Well ... there's nothing funny about it. But we act like it's such a great thing. No matter what side you are choosing, the president will drop bombs on people and innocent women and children will die. Let's say I have a friend in Afghanistan. Not a terrorist," I add. "He's minding his own business and working hard every day to earn a few dollars to provide food for himself in his hut. Let's say I practice my *civic duty*, the greatest thing about America. I elect an official who decides there's a terrorist group living by my friend that needs to be taken care of. My friend isn't a part of this group nor took part in any of their activities. Let alone knew of their existence. Our lovely President orders an F-117 to drop a cruise missile on them, but the calculations are slightly off. The missile does kill the terrorists but also kills my friend and a nearby family with three children. I technically just killed my friend and a family with children who did nothing wrong."

Mr. Hopper's jaw drops. The whole class stares back at me. For the first time, he doesn't reprimand me, say anything back, but awkwardly stutters about how the election will work. The majority wins, no electoral colleges here. But we do get to act as the "house."

Our election proceeds. The Republican Party wins, and I receive extra credit.

The most shocking part: Mr. Hopper didn't ask me to do push-ups for my digression.

Chapter 19

"I want many of you to do something different this week," Mr. Cannon says at the beginning of class.

"Most of you have been sticking to particular beats," he continues. "Mr. McCarthy aims for the slightly controversial rise. Mr. Burly covers everything sports related. This week I challenge some of you to switch beats," Mr. Cannon says. "I want us to do an issue on student life. This will require each of you to write a profile piece on a current student at Lakewood High."

I want to point out I *already* wrote on a different beat with my last article.

And I have no clue who I'll write a profile piece on.

"Mr. McCarthy, do you have any idea who you'll write about?" he asks me, staring.

"I can sit this week out. I already did the article on the Snow Coming Dance."

The class laughs. I'm a comedian.

"That will not be an option this week. Instead, think of it as an opportunity for even further growth."

"Can we write about a member of the faculty?" I ask. "If so, I'll write about Mr. Gensen and his cowboy boots."

The class laughs again.

"I think that one will only get you in more trouble, Mr. McCarthy. Let's leave this one to only students, but that's a good idea to have a staff featured issue in the future."

"I'd like the opportunity for one of my pieces to not be hit with heavy criticism by the administration." The words come out of my mouth before I can filter them. Sometimes this happens. It's like I think something and the next second there's a synapse, and my brain isn't fully communicating with my mouth and all the functions of my body.

"With words comes great responsibility," Mr. Cannon says. "Think of when the Patriot Act came out and the journalists reported illegal wiretapping. President Bush sat across from them and told them there would be blood on their hands if they printed the article. Because we have freedom of the press in this country, the president could not tell the newspaper not to run the article."

I'd like to point out the school does not have the same power granted in our constitution. This time I don't say this out loud.

"I know you may sometimes be under scrutiny," he pauses for what he hopes is dramatic emphasis. "But I want you to choose your words wisely. Have fun with your articles but think about how you affect others. Anyway, we have gotten off track."

Like Holden Caulfield, sometimes digressions are my favorite part of the day. Life is just a bunch of random events we as humans attach meaning to if you think about it, and for all we know, we don't really exist and are unwilling subjects to a wicked experiment and everything is an illusion.

Chapter 20

As you probably hypothesized by this point, I don't have any siblings. Mom and Pops never squirted out a bunch of kids in quick succession. Of course, I'd argue they had the one perfect child and realized no more were necessary.

Honestly, I *hate* being the only child. I wish I'd have another sibling to frame for crimes that occur, but as a result I am suspect Uno. Because of this, I've been conditioned to cover my tracks well.

The closest I probably have to a brother is our neighbor Tommy. He's about four or five years older than me and played with me every day during the summers when I was a kid. If I think about it, most of the kids I played with were older than me.

Think Pops decided to give me the whole "when a mommy loves a daddy" talk? Definitely not. Tommy filled me in as much as he could. Think I learned the hidden meaning behind the number 69 because of my high school education?

Or what the middle finger meant?

All Tommy.

I don't think he had all that much parental supervision either. Eventually, we ended up parting ways mainly because he got older and wanted to hang out with kids his age. He got girlfriends.

We occasionally still run into each other.

He introduced me to the band Tool. The video game *Mortal Combat*.

Last time I talked to him was after everything went down with Carmen.

"Hey," I said. "I need to talk to you."

"What's happening?" he asked. "Come on in."

"I need your help …"

It was kind of embarrassing to say it.

"About?"

"Girls."

"Ahh."

"Yeah."

"What seems to be troubling you?"

"I chatted for months with this one, Carmen, and then we went on a date. I thought everything was going good, and now she says she only wants to be friends."

"A date?" he looked at me.

"I took her to a movie."

"You don't want to take a girl on a date," he said, almost shaking his head. "You want to just *hang out* with girls."

"I thought a date made it sound like less of a friend thing."

"What'd you expect? Her to blow you in the theater?" Tommy let out a sigh. "See, you can't even talk much during a movie so sitting in silence watching something isn't going to make her like you more. You have to keep it casual. Even saying the word *date* puts pressure on the situation."

I thought about how he had his first girlfriend a few years before. She was a cute blonde.

"How do I tell if she likes me?"

"If she said she just wanted to be friends, she's probably not that into you. Sorry, I know that's hard to swallow."

"But she was. I could feel it. We both could."

"Chicks are like wild animals, man. They're unpredictable. Even if you're a certified trainer and in the cages with them, you still can't fully predict their behavior."

"Why not?"

"It's the way of women."

"How can I get her back?"

"There's no getting her back. She's either playing hot and cold with you, but it sounds more to me like she just lost interest. Or she found a better prospect."

"There has to be a way!" At this point I was desperate. Ready to tear out my eyes. The pain hurt worse than anything I'd felt in my life. I woke up regularly feeling like I was going to puke—and on a few occasions did—and like all the breath was taken from my lungs and I didn't know how to breath.

"Okay … Don't count on anything at all," Tommy looked at me, serious. "The only way you can get her back is to try not to get her back."

"What? That makes zero goddamn sense."

"Trust me. If you cling harder, chase her more, she will only run further away."

"Okay …"

"Make her come back to you. It's the only way."

And so … I took his advice, even though it was hard.

Chapter 21

We make "laws" for our "country." How it works: each person gets to propose a law, and then we vote on it. The "President" can either sign the bill into law or veto the bill. If he vetoes it, we—as "congress"—can take a vote, and if the vote is over 2/3, the bill becomes law.

It's all boring if you want to know the truth. I get it's supposed to teach us about democracy and all of that crap, but I'm just ready to take a goddamn nap.

Emma Bleer goes up in a cheery fashion. "I propose a law for a deposit on all water bottles for recycling and the environment."

Each time a person goes up they must start their sentence with "I propose."

Her bill passes. While we're not all very green, we can appreciate the simplicity of it and the sensibility.

I get this is supposed to make us feel more involved and get us excited about the idea of government and all, but to be honest, I think it just feels like one of those stupid simulations you do in middle school to demonstrate to kids what a free-market economy is like. And if we were 12, maybe this would be perfect, but, well, we're not . . .

"I propose . . ."

It's my turn. "I propose that we chop up all old people's licenses when they reach the age of 60. They are a menace to society with their slow driving, hitting mailboxes, running people over, and just not paying any attention. This is an issue I am passionate about. However, upon completion of a driver's training program, a driver may regain their license for up to three years with mandatory testing every three years to maintain this license."

"Mr. McCarthy, I don't know if I should ask you to do push-ups or not." Mr. Hopper eyes me, disapprovingly. A look I've become accustomed to.

"The next part of the bill would make it obligatory to ship every senior citizen past the age of 70 to a remote island so they don't bother the public. Here, they will drink coffee, talk about how things used to be, complain, watch Jeopardy, and play bingo."

The last part generates laughter from my peers.

"Do 15 push-ups for Karma, Mr. McCarthy."

My bill unanimously passes.

Other students come up and it becomes easy to zone out after a while. I'm reminded why I don't care for government all too much. Asides from the fact it's a bunch of idiots who lie every chance they get.

"I propose we legalize gay marriage," Avery Bowen, Lakewood High's first and only transgender student in probably the history of the school, says. "It's time things change and we accept love equally and all people equally."

"I knew Avery would be the first to say this shit," Ben Benson says in a voice only people in his nearby vicinity can hear. Since I'm lucky, I happen to be in the same proximity. He adds, "I have an amendment: we can legalize gay marriage, but we should put all of them on a boat, steer this boat into the middle of Lake Michigan, then proceed to sink this boat as they are a disgrace to the human race."

"Jesus," I say.

"Do you have something to add Mr. McCarthy?" Mr. Hopper asks.

"Sorry."

The president vetoes the vote. I elicit no surprise from the decision.

"Before we take a house vote, I'm going to let other people speak on the matter. Who else proposed to legalize gay marriage?" Mr. Hopper asks.

Five others raise their hands.

"I'd like to speak on the matter," Benson says.

Benson clears his throat in his cheesy over-the-top sort of way. "This is the type of matter that the older generations look at us and talk about. It's not an issue of rights; it's a moral issue. Legalizing gay marriage is a slippery slope. They say they were *born this way*. Is that honestly going to be the defense everybody can use? Next, we won't be able to stop bank robbers as they're robbing a bank because they'll say, *I was born thief!*"

"I want to speak on the matter," I say.

"One second, Mr. McCarthy, I believe Mr. Benson is still talking, and we have two other volunteers ahead of you."

"God created Adam and Eve, not Adam and Steve," Benson continues. "It's just unnatural."

Sarah James comes to the front of the class next.

"What Ben said is right," Sarah James says. "It says in the Bible that gay marriage is wrong. We need to vote against it."

"Guys this is all wrong. It doesn't say anywhere in Bible that gay marriage is immoral," Sam Montly says. "It's just not right."

I'm up. "First off, my members of congress, I want to tell you that 1.) This is not a moral issue. It's subjective. I'm no criminal expert, but I don't think a man putting his tongue in another man's mouth is the same as robbing a bank. As for my fellow men in here, do you think it's the same when a girl sticks her tongue in another girl's mouth?"

This generates some laughter and a stern look from Mr. Hopper.

"I'd also like to point out that God did not create Adam and Eve. In fact, I'd argue there is no God; therefore, He didn't create anything. Do we really believe we're all the products of incest? Think about it. Besides we have to separate Church and State."

Looking out I see it's a tough crowd on this one. Everybody is taught to believe in *some* form of Christianity. Even if they don't go to church every weekend, or only conveniently mention the powers of a mythical deity when it suits their views of an afterlife or promotes another facet of their agenda.

"Who honestly cares what it says in some book that was written thousands of years ago by people who don't live in the world we live in? I mean it's just people talking about their imaginary friend. In America, our imaginary friend tells us to ban gay marriage. In Islam, their imaginary friend tells them to fly planes into buildings. It's all completely fictional. We can't just deny other's rights because Christians don't want it. And besides, are you honestly going to tell me we should follow a book that not only openly endorses slavery but promotes violence against slaves?"

The class is silent. Sarah James looks like she's about to burst into tears. Sam Montly looks uneasy. Benson sneers at me. Mr. Hopper looks on like he's watching his favorite porno. He can really get off on all the debate stuff.

We vote and gay marriage fails in our society by a 60% to 40% vote.

After class Avery Bowen grabs my arm as I walk by. "I appreciate what you said," he says. He used to be a target for constant ridicule because he used to be she and is currently undergoing modifications but legally can't get surgery done until 18. Because of his good sense of humor, most people have stopped making fun of him. On top of it: he is one of the nicest people you will ever meet.

"No problem," I say. "I did it more for me than for you."

"Well, it helps my cause," Avery says. "And it means a lot to me."

Chapter 22

Carmen stands by my locker. Occasionally, she surprises me. But because of her unpredictable nature, I never count on her to visit me anywhere during school hours. She's quite gregarious, talking with numerous people—both guys and gals—and never stays in a set pattern I've deciphered.

"I heard about the uproar."

"The what?"

"You and your political debates. Oh, and your hatred for the elderly."

"I thought it was a reasonable proposition."

Carmen tries holding back a smile but fails.

"I heard you were a communist as well."

I laugh and can't help it. "More like an anarchist."

"I heard the whole class was silent and you went on a rant the other day."

I shrug.

"You never care about winning anybody over."

"That's not true."

It lingers in the air. She looks down, I force eye contact. The unspoken failed attempt and my lack of wooing ability, the fact I'm friendship material but not relationship material in her eyes.

"You know who you should write about for your article?"

"It's going to be my article, so back off, lady."

I expect a farfetched idea to come out of her mouth.

"Write it on Avery Bowen."

I look at Carmen, trying to gage her level of seriousness.

"It will piss so many people off. Think of all the people in your government class. Think about all of these tight-ass closed-minded people."

"I don't know if he's article worthy."

I don't want to write an article on anybody. Once I wrote about Hitler when I had Miss Fett, a bubbly blonde English teacher, who encouraged us to write about an inspirational person for a paper. This resulted in a trip to Mr. Gensen's office. I followed this up with a paper where we answered the difficult question, "Is charity good?" I argued charity is bad. If people died because of the lack of food, this would only create more elbow space. People ignore their friends, family, and children right in front of them, failing them, but enrich stranger's lives rather than those in their nearby vicinity, and most of all people only perform charity work to feel good about *themselves*; it's not about the actual people they supposedly "help."

"He is. Believe me. Think about Ben Benson. Think about bringing attention to an issue nobody wants to talk about or acknowledge."

"Does Avery even want to be put in the spotlight like that?"

"I think if Avery was put in the right light, he would." Carmen says. "And, I mean, he is running for Snow Coming King."

"I'll think about it."

"I need a ride home," she says.

Chapter 23

The second we exit the school building, Carmen says, "Let's not go to my home right away. Let's go for a drive."

"Where are we going?" I ask.

"Nowhere in particular, just drive," she commands. "My dad took my car. I want to go for a ride."

I make sure to remember everything taught in driver's training and by Gramps. I check my blind spots. I ensure my hands are in a 3 and 9 o'clock grip on the steering wheel. One time in driver's training they made us watch an entire video titled, "Don't Race Trains." We spent a whole goddamn hour being informed not to attempt to race a train to the tracks or stop on the tracks. No new information was presented that couldn't have been deciphered from the title. The outcome: chances are if your vehicle gets hits by a train, it will end poorly.

"Don't you want me to take you home?"

"I just want to go for a ride."

"Drive around town?"

"Take the highway."

I've always dreamed about just taking the highway and leaving the Skee. Taking I-94 south and never looking back.

"If you could go anywhere in the world, where would you go?" Carmen breaks the silence after a few minutes.

Carmen and I are playing this game where she'll keep asking me questions, probing at answers. This is a mild version of the game.

"Nowhere."

Carmen and I keep driving in my car, going nowhere in particular.

"There has to be somewhere."

She rests her hand on my leg, warm.

"Anywhere but here."

"That's a copout answer."

"You know we both haven't been outside of the country."

A painful fact.

"But you have to have like a place you want to go?"

I settle for a moment of honesty. "A tropical island with crystal clear beaches, not a drop of pollution in the water and no cigarette buds in the sand. Just clear beaches and crystal clear water as far as the eye can see. I want it desolate. No people."

"What country would that be?"

"Probably no country in existence."

We drive. All the streets are familiar.

Carmen's hand massages my leg, soothing yet exiting at the same time. Carmen thinks for a second and stares out the window looking nowhere in particular. Crazy travel plans ping through her brain. Even though I've probably heard them all, I want to hear her tell me about them again.

I don't say anything. The silence permeates. Finally, I ask, "Where did you used to live anyway?"

"Before I moved here at the start of my freshman year, I lived in this small town in Indiana along the border. It was this janky town with a bunch of meth heads, crack was abundant, a high birth rate, and tons of poverty. It wasn't the worst town and for a while things seemed alright. Then it started. Every night my parents would scream at each other. It came to the point where if they wouldn't for just one day, it was abnormal. I'd dread hearing the sound of my dad's pickup truck pull into the driveway every day after he got home from the factory. I knew the fighting would start. Most of the time we didn't even make it to dinner before they started fighting."

I'm silent for a second.

"Whatever happened to your mom?" Carmen asks out of nowhere.

I shrug.

"You never talk about it."

"To be honest, I don't know."

"You don't know?" Carmen looks at me like I'm crazy.

"Meaning something happened where my dad and her didn't get along, but he never told me what."

Carmen keeps staring at me. "That's odd ... do you have any memories of her?"

"When I was three or four, we went on this trip to the ocean. We drove there and I behaved the entire way. The ocean looked kind of like Lake Michigan, even though it's bigger. I don't remember much, but I remember some of it. We built a sandcastle on the beach and played in the water. We ate elephant ears as we walked the beach. It's the only time I've ever been out of Michigan."

Chapter 24

Cheating is a necessary part of high school. Some students are naturally gifted and have no reason to cheat. This is great for them. But I'm not one of these students. I've tried memorizing formulas, only to have them vanish the second the test is in front of me. This is why cheat sheets are a necessary mastery I've perfected since freshman year.

The trick is to write small. *Very* small. Almost illegibly small to the point it'd be a size six in Microsoft Word. Of course, you can type out the words too, but I'm a bigger fan of the smaller handwriting on a small sheet of paper. One that will fit inside your sleeve.

I'm putting the finishing touches on my cheat sheet for Pre-Calc when I realize Mr. Laurel is standing right behind me.

"What do you got there?" Mr. Laurel asks.

My whole body freezes. Per rules set out at the beginning of the year—cheating in any form on any test or assignment—I'm getting a zero on the test.

"Is that your little cheat sheet?"

I turn and look him right in the eye.

"Yes, it is," I say.

He laughs and pats me on the back, like I said a funny joke.

I proceed to use the cheat sheet on the test.

The next day—it's like all of the teachers talked and decided to have all of the tests the same week—I have a test in Physics. This one is worse; I don't even know where to *begin* to make a cheat sheet, because I understand nothing about the class.

Luckily, Kenzinger helps assist me during tests at times, making his answers clearly visible. Overall, he's a far better student than me and understands the stuff. We're supposed to show our work. Creating identical tests is never a good idea. I omit some of what he writes, write down other nonsensical things, and make it the same but different. I copy his entire test. Thankfully, I manage to decipher his handwriting, but I have practice.

I've noticed a direct correlation between how neat a person's handwriting is and their overall intelligence. Take for example, Matt Dallop, one of the brightest minds our school has to offer, kids refer to his writing as "chicken scratch." Kenzinger's is slightly better but not by much. And this other kid, Alan McElson, his handwriting is the neatest you'll ever see—especially for a guy's—but most rocks possess more intelligence than him.

By the time I get to the essay question, I stop copying. There is a certain art to skillful copying.

He writes an entire goddamn essay with many paragraphs on the four-point essay question; I accept I'll be docked the four points for it and settle on only writing one sentence.

Throughout my high school career, I've shared answers frequently. At one point freshman year—we had a substitute teacher for the remainder of the year in history—we not only had an open book exam but were unofficially allowed to debate answers amongst ourselves.

I would have never made it past Spanish if it was not for glancing at other people's papers or for creating carefully planned cheat sheets in my glasses' case during class. The truth is I didn't even *need* my glasses to see close up, but during every class I'd take them out during the tests with my cheat sheets taped to the case. (I only survived one year of Spanish before deciding not to take any more.)

During Geography class, sophomore year, I'd make sure to have my folder out on the map below my desk. It's important to always have something on top of it, not be blatantly obvious by staring at the floor, and to be quick about it. Like most Americans when it comes to geography, I don't have the slightest goddamn idea where anything is located.

My collaborative spirit in finding answers traces back to elementary school the first time we were given free rein in labs. As a result, I have a knack for asking other people for answers, filling in the blanks, finding out who knows what and is good at what—all while bringing relatively little to the table myself.

I've yet to get busted in my high school career for cheating. I get myself into enough trouble as it is, so I think it's for the best my record remains unscathed in this area.

I mean, the truth is, all the time I've spent creating cheat sheets I could have probably studied in the first place.

Chapter 25

People always ask the same questions. People will ask, "How are you doing?" without caring what the answer is. It's all a charade.

People will say, "nice to meet" you before they even know who you are and if it was in fact nice to meet you. I refrain from either cliché.

After a while the monotony of the school year fades together but in different shifts. The seasons pass, everything stays the same but different. First, a nervous anticipation filled me of never knowing what to expect, but that wore off. Then, it was waiting for the year to fly by, but it doesn't happen how you expect it to.

I make a habit of avoiding too many rituals—although certain ones such as senior pranks are mandatory every year—and mixing up my routine. Walking different routes in school. Each attempt at avoiding this purgatory existence and escaping perpetual boredom fails miserably, leaving me only to find ways to escape it.

"Want to go to the church?" Carmen asks me, appearing out of nowhere—generally, I'm well aware of her presence in any hallway, regardless of how close she is to me; her legs are like magnets and my eyes are glued to them.

"I've already prayed today."

Carmen looks at me without breaking eye contact and I look away.

Even back when my dad went to school, students always gathered across the street before school started, during lunch breaks, and after school. While I could say these students are adamant about their worship and want to have God in their lives every single day, that would be a lie.

It's the common gathering place where students smoke, whether it's cigarettes or pot.

"You know why."

"I'm not in the mood to make out with you."

"I wouldn't want you to fall in love with me."

"Like I ever would." Sometimes lying is a necessity when it comes to girls; females are a species I've failed to decipher. I know when I actually *acted* interested in Carmen, she wasn't interested in me. Now that I appear more indifferent, she's willing to show up and initiate conversations with me.

Every time she looks at me, I feel like she sees through me.

"I have bud," she offers. She's more of a dope fiend than me.

"You're a bad influence. You want me to skip school to smoke?"

Carmen smiles oddly, exposing her crooked tooth she claims makes her smile look "janky"—which I insist only adds character and depth. Her eyes twinkle at me, those blue disks sucking me in like black holes, and I know I would agree to any minor request, and I hate myself for lacking restraint.

Once we exit the school, Carmen stops. "Okay, I led you here under false pretenses," she begins.

"We're going to do dirty things?"

"Better!"

"Your friend Alexis is going to join?"

"Hey," she smacks my arm harder than she normally does. "I didn't score reefer, but I have these." She holds up a bag and I swear her mischievous eyes twinkle turning from sapphire to admiral blue.

What she holds up looks like shriveled-up mushrooms. "I don't like mushrooms."

"Nobody likes the taste of them."

"What do you expect here?"

"We're going to have an experience."

"Why don't you do it with one of your other friends?"

"I want to do it with you."

"You're such a druggie. I was this good kid before you, and you've completely corrupted me."

"That's a lie. You thought about trying things and you were perverted before. I helped free you and appreciate the gray areas in life a little more."

"Where are we going to possibly do this?"

"My dad and stepmom are gone for the weekend."

Chapter 26

Carmen's house rests across the line separating the west and east side of the city. The east side is called Muskegon Heights. While Carmen's house is only a few blocks into the heights, I make sure to lock my doors—as she told me to do—when I exit my car.

My peers tell stories. Drug stories and drinking stories. Which means despite my lack of hands-on experience, I have heard quite a bit about mushrooms. I've heard stories of people melting before your eyes, mythical animals appearing, and the general loss of reality.

We chew on the mushrooms which taste like health food I once ate at Sarah Martin's house when I stopped by sophomore year for a project and her mom gave us breakfast bars.

"These are disgusting." Carmen wrinkles her mouth and scrunches her nose.

"It was your idea."

After we chew the disgustingly unhygienic—mind you these grew on cow shit—fungus, we wait. I stare at the walls expecting them to close in around me, and a blur of psychedelics to impede my vision.

"I feel nothing," I say.

Carmen runs her fingers around the couch we're sitting on. "You're the only guy I've taken back to my place, unsupervised."

The last part hits me in the chest and the first part makes me ponder the implications of *unsupervised*.

"Have you taken any other guys back to your place?"

"No. And you're the only one my dad's ever met."

"You mean the only guy ever?"

"Yes." She nods with such sincerity I know it's true. For some obtuse reason the confidence in knowing I'm the only one she's introduced to her dad flows through me.

Over the next half hour our conversations shift. In the next few hours:

1.) I feel too hot and too cold. As a result, I take my T-shirt on and off five times in the first hour.

2.) I notice how everybody is smiling, not smiling, or looking apprehensive in pictures. And the carpet feels so soft under my feet.

3.) Carmen gets too hot and takes off her shirt (she has a bra underneath) which should draw attention to the fact both of us are on drugs. She takes her shirt on and off over the next few hours three times.

4.) We discover a perfect medium of warmth with our skin pressed against each other. She feels soft like a perfume you try to savor but can't absorb the entirety of.

5.) We notice the textures of the walls. Marks on the floor we haven't before.

6.) We listen to as much music as we can.

7.) I have moments of clarity even though it feels like insects are running through my head. I'll ask myself questions like: *Do I really like Carmen?* The answer: yes. *Should I write an article on Avery?* Undeniable answer: yes.

8.) Nothing happens but I still recall Carmen's purple bra and the circular patterns on it, the patterns in the floor, and my need to write a damn good newspaper article.

9.) After a few hours things go back to normal, but I feel changed somehow, even if in a small subtle way, but I don't feel like I can rationally justify how or why.

Chapter 27

Carmen and I watch T.V. the next morning. I slept on her couch.

"What kind of porn do you watch?" she asks me for about the third time.

"I don't watch porn, really." I lie for the third time.

"There's that *really* in there which implies a minute amount at the very least. Unless, of course ... you're lying." She says the last two words the loudest, and I'm thankful this is a private conversation in the confines of her home.

"I know you want a blow job. It's like the idea had to come from *somewhere*," she says. Normally, we only message this type of stuff over AIM, but occasionally she slips up in real life—it's weird thinking of us having different mediums, an Online Me and an Online Carmen, and I wonder if we project more to each other online, which is messed up since real life should be better, but online feels easier; there's no initial judgments just open dialogues.

I let the silence fill the room. While I appreciate her overall interest in the subject of oral sex—perhaps her fixation even—sometimes when she drills me on it, I don't know what to say. And the obvious truth always emerges; I have yet to have full hands-on experience on the subject. For now, it's only my imagination.

"Like how does somebody honestly have the idea to stick their penis in somebody's mouth out of nowhere?"

"You'd be surprised," I blurt out.

"Would I?" She arches an eyebrow at me and doesn't break eye contact, meaning for some reason I can't break eye contact, even though I feel my cheeks becoming red and my heart rate elevates.

"It's that age-old question of which came first, the chicken or the egg? Did I start thinking of blow jobs after watching porn or did I think of it, then confirm it with porn? I don't remember."

This last part is the truth. I never dreamed of being celibate or waiting until marriage, but it's not like I have it all figured out. Sometimes I wish Carmen would help me figure it out and we could explore together. Of course, this part was already implied when I tried *dating* her and the entire school knows how that went. (Or at least I thought they did; now I'm not sure. Some people know certain things but even her close friends don't know everything.)

Chapter 28

As previously stated, I'm forced to visit my Gramps for dinner with my father at least once a month if not every other week. Thankfully, in the winter, with all the tremendous amounts of snow, sometimes we get a real storm—at least three feet of snow—making this too tedious for even my old man.

Instead of cooking, Gramps decided to order a pizza. At least it's not soup. That's one meal I can't stand. It's only for old people. I still have teeth to chew my food, so there's no reason for me to eat soup. Of course, Gramps loves it. I'll wait until I'm in a nursing home to start eating soup.

Generally, Gramps sits in his old chair, this gray one that rocks and reclines that's probably older than I am—I mean I remember it being there for as long as I can remember—watching TV. If he's not watching Jeopardy, he's watching the news.

The news comes on with the words "immigration."

"I wish we'd stop letting all of these people in," Gramps says. "They come over here and steal American jobs."

He could go on and on about how America is "The Greatest Country in the World" even though he rarely leaves the Skee and has never even been out of the country mind you. It's not like I have either, but I at least know there's a world out there. I can tell you, if the Skee is the greatest city in the world, then the world does suck.

The news comes on, and I zone out.

"We should stop letting all of these Mexicans into our country."

I should give him points for saying "Mexicans" instead of "beaners" this time.

"We need to get rid of them as soon as we can and take them back to their own country. We just need to start shipping them out right now. They're no good for America."

Finally, I speak up. "You do realize they work jobs that most Americans don't want, right? For example, picking blueberries in the fields for $2 an hour. Not many Americans would jump at that splendid opportunity."

Gramps looks at me like he wants to administer physical discipline that is no longer allowed in this generation.

"They take good American jobs, and they should just stay in their own damn country." I remember one time a Black couple moved in across the street. Talk about a rough day in the office for Gramps sitting in his recliner. It ruined his entire day. "I can't believe they're letting all these Blacks move into the neighborhood," he said.

The pizza finally arrives.

We sit at the table.

"Take off your hat," Gramps commands me. "It's rude to have your hat on at the table."

A courtesy my dad has never enforced.

Begrudgingly, I remove my warm cap from my head. It's actually a pretty cool hat, one of those older ones that has two flaps on it and a warm interior, a red plaid pattern on it, perfect for Michigan winters.

"Thank you, Lord, for providing this meal before us," Gramps says. "Keep us safe and healthy. Amen."

He doesn't mention anything about the pizza place preparing the pizza for us or the delivery driver driving on the icy roads or the fact that He didn't have anything to do with it, but I decide I'm too hungry to wage another war.

Unfortunately, Gramps only ordered deluxe. I pick off the unnecessary ingredients that will tarnish the pizza. Meaning everything except pepperoni.

"Why are you wasting food?" Gramps asks.

"I only like pepperoni."

He scoffs, debating going into a story about how back in World War II food was scarce and how when he was a kid, he was required to eat every morsel of food in front of him or else he'd have to sit at the table until he was finished, and if he didn't finish it, the food would be breakfast the next morning.

"You need a haircut," he tells me. He always tells me this.

"I like it longer," I say between bites.

Gramps and I used to feed ducks. My dad used to hate it. It sounds random, but every week my grandpa would take me down by Lake Harbor. We'd go by the channel separating Mona Lake from Lake Michigan, and he'd give me bread. I'd toss it to the ducks. I'd be obsessed with it, watching as they swam closer, gobbling up the bread, diving underwater.

"You're not supposed to feed the ducks," Pops said. "It's not good for them." Pops adamantly hated the feeding of any wild animals because it made them "reliant on human food" rather than going into their natural environment for food. Plus, with birds, he'd say it made them congregate and "shit everywhere." He told me this when I was five.

"Let him feed the damn ducks," Gramps would say.

He'd hand me another piece of bread. It sounds stupid, but for a kid it was the best thing in the world. The only time I ever fed the ducks was with Gramps.

For some reason, Pops always caved, and we always fed the ducks.

"You know, you can always come back to church," Gramps says, directing this at my dad. We *used* to do the whole church thing with my grandpa until I was ten. I'm not going to lie and act like we went every Sunday or anything like that, or I regularly was a part of after school church groups, but we still went. It kind of trickled off after a bit. I know it made Gramps happy and all since he went to the same church, but I knew since I was 12 that it wasn't my jam and I preferred sleeping in on Sunday. And I didn't want to go to a building with a million old people in it, kids running around screaming their goddamn heads off, watching as they passed around trays for money since God always bums off of everybody and never quite figured out the money thing, and listen to these god-awful songs week after week.

It's not like I *blame* God for not wanting to balance a checkbook. One time my Economics teacher, Mr. Carter, taught us how. Talk about a mind-numbing skill I never want to use, but he assured us it would be necessary to "manage our finances" in the future.

My dad chews his food and looks down.

"It's a drive for us," Pops says. "And there's more homework now and writing for the school newspaper."

"It's only an hour service. One hour of your time. God needs you there."

Which, in all honesty, is a weird thing to say. God is supposed to be everywhere, but he needs us in that building for some reason every Sunday listening to old people talk while drinking coffee and eating donuts.

"I'm getting another slice of pizza." Pops gets up from the table.

"Don't you miss church?" Gramps asks me. It's like asking me if I miss having a nail in my foot.

If I talked to any other imaginary person, people would start to get worried about me. They'd think I developed schizophrenia. Religion is mass schizophrenia. A shared wide-held belief having no basis in reality.

But because it's a wide-held belief in West Michigan, I'm made out to be the weird one.

"Not really," I say, trying not to argue.

"I miss having both of you there, and you're welcome to come anytime."

We make exceptions for the holidays. We went on Christmas Eve. Sometimes we go on Easter.

"We got a new pastor," he informs my dad when he sits back down. They've had three new ones—well, four now—since our old one, Pastor Eric, split after cheating on his wife. He had an affair with a younger gal studying under him (no pun intended). I remember all the sermons he taught around that time; one was how happy he was that his wife accepted his marriage proposal and how important the vows of marriage are.

Strictly, a load of crap, having to listen to that hypocrite up there telling me how to live my life when he refused to hold himself to the same standards.

When it was publicly known to the congregation that he was having an affair, Gramp said, "Well, the first question everybody had to ask: was it a woman or a man? We all know how liberal he is."

I couldn't help but feel sorry for his wife. I mean she was a good-looking woman for her age.

So, Pastor Eric left after the whole affair, relocated with his wife to another town to start over. I guess she must have forgiven him.

Well, after they relocated to a new town, he did it *again*. With a different woman. We were told last year they found his body floating in Lake Michigan, in a suit, fully clothed. Suicide. While I'm not for suicide—you have to be in a pretty awful place to want to just end it all; although admittedly, I've been there (mostly when all of the stuff with Carmen took place)—I think there are certain circumstances where it's a relief. I imagine him doing the same thing at the next church and the one after that and the cycle would keep repeating driving his wife crazy. So, in this instance, I think it's a good thing he decided to resign from life. Maybe suicide was noble in this case.

"Try to look alive," Gramps says to me. The irony.

I don't point out that he looks like a corpse at this point.

Chapter 29

"What are you doing for your government project?" Kenzinger asks me when I sit down. We're supposed to shadow a "government worker" for the day. It only has to be for four hours, and then we have to write up a goddamn report about the experience.

Mr. Hopper did say, "If you need assistance finding somebody to shadow for a day, I have plenty of people to connect you with."

"I was going to practice the art of bullshit," I say.

I'm brought back to when I took an introductory psych course and we were supposed to watch people. She told us it could be anywhere of our choosing. Instead of actually doing the assignment, I made up the entire thing about going to the food court in the mall and watching what people ordered at the Chinese place. My teacher thought my paper was good and detailed and read it to the entire class. I didn't have the heart to tell her I made up the entire thing.

I wonder if some journalists do this.

Also, if you want to make anything sound more official just add the phrase, "based on a study by [insert name of University here]." The trick is to not name *too* prestigious of a university, such as Harvard or Yale, but say something like Duke University or Michigan State University.

We were told to never use Wikipedia because it's unreliable. Apparently, our teachers made their own page about the awesomeness of Lakewood High teachers to demonstrate this point. This just means that most of us change the name of the source when using Wikipedia.

"My parents said they know somebody you can shadow," he says.

Doing the assignment correctly was not an option I considered. "I don't want to be an inconvenience. They don't need to go out of their way."

While I do provide rides three times a week, I never feel like he owes me anything. And, besides, he shares his answers quite frequently.

"My mom already contacted somebody."

Kenzinger pulls through in clutch situations. I thought that weekend would consist of me bullshitting an entire job shadow I didn't do, forging signatures for the paperwork.

"I have a new project for you," Mr. West announces. "It's another hands-on project." He appears visibly excited as he says this. Earlier in the year, we had to make a car designed to go by the sole power of a mousetrap. To be honest, Pops did the entire car thing as I watched, having no desire to participate.

"We're going to make a flying device out of straws and yarn. The goal is to protect this." He produces an egg. "From cracking when it is dropped from the top of the bleachers in the football stadium."

"You're welcome to come to the front of the class to check out examples."

Nobody moves.

"Well, come on. These are worth checking out." Mr. West motions with an exciting big stupid grin on his face, not realizing the inconvenience such a project will cause me.

We get our tests back.

Kenzinger got 27 out of 30.

I received a 30.

The points that were deducted from his paper were for the essay question. Only one point. I received four full points for my sentence. I quickly put the test away, because I don't want him to see it.

Chapter 30

Before Government begins, I run into Avery.

"Hey, I was looking for you."

"Yeah?" He looks at me. His hair is blonde and cut short. Everybody gets confused by if it's "he" or "she," and as a result, Avery has become the burden of many cruel jokes and comments about "a dickless dude." Some call Avery "it." Others simply say, they don't understand. I may be one of the people that don't understand, but I've never once muttered a cruel insult. In a way, I think people should be allowed to do whatever the hell they want, as long as they're not bringing assault rifles to school, assembling bombs, hurting anybody, or planning to.

"I'm writing an article and have to do a student profile," I begin. "I thought you'd be an optimal candidate to express the diversity of the student body."

Avery laughs. "Are you serious?"

"100%. I mean I could just interview somebody on one of our sports teams and feel myself lose brain cells?"

"This isn't some kind of joke, is it? You're not just going to make me out to be some freak?"

Avery glares at me, defensively. A spark under his eyes.

"The thought never occurred to me. Besides, this might be a good way to promote yourself, make your side of the story known if say you were going to ..."

"... Run for Snow Coming King?"

"Something like that."

"Everybody talks so much here."

"It's just word on the street. Besides, I think it's a great idea. I mean I'll vote for you." The truth is I honestly couldn't care less who wins, but if it's going to make people like Sarah James cry or Benson feel like someone pissed in his shoes then I am all for it.

"It's not because you love to stick to non-controversial articles that do little to provoke anybody?"

"I like to rile people up. The thought of Benson having a hemorrhage reading it does make me satisfied. I mean this is your chance to say what you want to say. Nobody telling you no. Nobody telling you that you're wrong."

"There's more to me than only switching sides and causing a big uproar. It's all anybody wants to talk about when they talk about me."

"I want the full picture. A well-rounded story."

A true profile piece.

Mr. Cannon told us in most cases we must search for balance in an article to be fair—show both sides of the stories, even if someone is a complete jerk at least let them defend themselves, which I suppose is fair. However, when doing a profile piece, he said it's okay not to "unbury any corpses." It's about letting the readers connect with somebody, whether through their hobbies, points of view, or general interests.

"You better not make me the butt of some joke." Avery says this dead serious. Maybe all the teasing, ridicule, and name-calling has gotten to Avery more than I realized.

He seems so strong-willed and unshakeable always. Confident in who Avery is.

"You've always seemed confident in who you are."

"Thanks. I mean I've had backing by some important people, but not everybody is on my team. I have my doubts."

"This is our chance to get everybody on Team Avery. Plus, you're going to run for Snow Coming King, so don't you think giving you some hype before the vote would help you out?"

Chapter 31

In Women and Minorities, we're supposed to read one article each week on either a women or minority issue. Most of us had no clue where to look. While we're encouraged to take notes, Mr. Gardner says as long as we can talk about it in class that will suffice.

Last week as Alex and I were sitting at computers in the library, Mr. Gardner came up to us. "I can give you suggestions for articles. Here, read this one." He said to Alex, handing him a piece of paper.

I read the article.

"Let's share the articles we read last week," Mr. Gardner says. "We'll start with Alex. Please share the article you read last week."

"I ... ehhh ... didn't get to it." Alex says.

"It was about driving while Black,'" I say. "Police officers will pull over people of different races for the sole reason they belong to a particular race. 'Driving while Black' pinpoints instances of police pulling over African Americans, Black people, I mean, for no reason other than their skin color. One particular instance was Ray Smith in this article on November 6, 2006. He didn't have any drugs in his system or any alcohol. But the police officer insisted that he needed to search his car, which I'd like to point out is illegal without permission or a warrant."

"I gave the article to you," Mr. Gardner points to Alex. "But you read it instead?"

I nod.

Mr. Gardner looks at me with approval.

"This is common occurrence where people who are Black or of other races are pulled over strictly for their skin color," Mr. Gardner says. "A police officer is supposed to have a valid reason for pulling a car over by law; he can't just pull somebody over for fun."

"Somebody forgot what it's like being a teenager," I mutter. Alex laughs.

Mr. Gardner shoots me a look, and I shut up instantly.

We break off into group activities.

Before the end of class, Jerry gets up. Of course, we're experiencing that juxtapose where all of our things are at the others seat, and we didn't take all of our stuff with us when we moved. He sits halfway across the classroom normally.

Jim Green, the high school quarterback, who is a nice kid—he was my partner in driver's training—is in Jerry's seat.

"Hey, Green, can you throw me my agenda book?" Jerry yells. "Oh, wait. Never mind, you won't be able to hit me with it anyway."

He walks to the other side of the room and grabs it.

Chapter 32

Carmen and I people watch sometimes. We're in the Big Lakes mall. It's more inland and doesn't hug the lake like our normal part of town. It's in the middle of a bunch of restaurants. It has the normal stores in it: Hollister, American Eagle, JCPenny, FYE, Hot Topic, and a boring store with a bunch of smelly candles.

We're eating cinnamon rolls at Auntie Anne's in the food court.

"What do you think their story is?" Carmen asks.

There's a cute couple, a guy and a girl our age. The girl has straight black hair and brown eyes, and the guy looks like he came out of a Hollister catalogue with his spiked dyed blond hair, skin-tight polo shirt, and ripped faded jeans.

On second thought, I think they look a little older.

"I bet they were high school sweethearts," Carmen says.

"They're probably a happy couple." I imagine the life Carmen and I could have. "But they don't realize how miserable they should be. She'll probably leave him the second she changes her mind, which she does by the minute. Either to find another guy or just at will."

Carmen looks at me.

"Or maybe she doesn't want to just be another notch on his bedpost. A conquest he pursued hard only to lose interest a week later after he put in that month of effort convincing her what a good guy he is and how he isn't like all the other guys."

Other people walk around the food court in the mall. Mostly couples. Some have children in strollers.

"Or maybe they're actually a happy couple and don't fight each other constantly."

"Because peace is so interesting ..." Carmen lets out an audible sigh.

"I'm sure our forefathers agree ... fighting for independence was so interesting. That's the reason they did it. Or we fought in World War II because it seems like such an exciting conflict to be involved in—"

"What about after the happy-ever-after, then what?"

I don't know what to say. A chance at forming something. A sense of being with someone. Knowing you're not the only one in the world to feel like you do. You know you've found someone. Not just someone, but the person you're meant to be with, who you feel like you belong with. Even if in a way you question it too, and you doubt they feel the same way about you, but no matter what you're not giving up on this feeling, this thought, this desire. You know this person could make you happier than anybody else. And you think you could too.

I take a bite of my cinnamon roll.

"Exactly, a conquest." Carmen smirks.

"You don't understand everything you know."

We walk for a bit. Carmen walks closer than normal to me, brushing into me. We go through the normal stores.

Explore the goth extremes of Hot Topic. Screamo music blares from their speakers. The clothing is only black.

We explore the preppy stores. Carmen wears some of the clothes but not all of it.

"How about we find you a nice shirt?" she suggests. Carmen explores the boy's aisle. Polo shirts and collared shirts galore.

"You mean one with a nice collar on it?"

"Why not?"

"That's something a girlfriend would do. Dress up her boyfriend how she wants him to look."

"Or I can find you nicer pants, so you can stop wearing cargo pants," she says.

"Don't hate."

She grabs three shirts from the girl's section.

"How many?" the person in charge of the fitting room asks.

"Two," Carmen says.

"Didn't you—"

Carmen shoots me a look.

We leave the store.

"What did you do?" I ask.

We're walking to the parking lot.

"You like to borrow answers. Sometimes I borrow clothes." She pulls out a shirt.

"You mean steal. Borrow with no intention of giving back. At least when I say borrow answers it's accurate. Or share answers. The person still has their own."

"Not everybody has money."

Chapter 33

We meet at "Erman Owling Enter" according to the sign whose "S," "H," "B," and "C" are dead and haven't been replaced in years. At one time in my youth the sign read, "Sherman Bowling Center," but nobody cared enough to replace the lettering in the sign.

Avery chose the setting for the interview. I asked Avery to get coffee, but he said he doesn't drink coffee. While I understand this thought process, I can't fathom not having a warm caffeinated beverage in the morning. "The interview has to be off of school grounds," Avery insisted.

Which leads us here: a run-down bowling center that's been here since bowling was invented. Aside from the missing letters in the sign, the carpet could be replaced, and it smells like cigarettes. But it's fairly cheap; this Friday it's three games for $3.

"I don't bowl," I say.

Avery snorts. "I don't either, but it's an opportunity to smoke cigarettes inside where nobody will ID you or care if you're old enough."

My face must reveal my surprise.

"You didn't know I smoke?"

"I can't say I did." Before writing a piece on somebody, it's important to think about what you know about the person. In my case, it's all word on the street. People label Avery as "a freak," "confused," a "he-she," but I know none of the story behind his life.

His friend, Dustin, is coming to join us in half an hour. Thinking about it, I really don't know much about him either, and many people fall in the cracks here at our school. People I've had classes with in middle school who I never see again. People who I "know"—meaning I know their name and basic information about them but absolutely nothing else.

Carmen is coming in half an hour as well. Enough time Avery and I deem to conduct the interview while still having a night.

"Do you want a cigarette?" Avery asks.

I look around but then remember where I am.

"They never ID anyone here," he repeats. "They don't care."

"I'll take one." When in Rome.

"So let's begin ..." To make a good profile interview first you need the basics. I confirm all the "housekeeping" shit Mr. Cannon referred to. Next, ask probing questions. Ask open-ended questions after "housekeeping." Not yes or no, questions. Say things like, "Tell me about it."

I learn Avery's circle of friends changes continually.

"One of the most difficult things was finding a solid support system in all this," Avery says. "People would be my friend one day then turn on me the next. It made me very depressed for a long time."

"Do you feel like you have a support system now?"

"Yes, I do. It's not like in middle school or the beginning of high school. My therapist told me I need to keep trying to reach more people so I won't feel—" Avery stops mid-sentence and looks at me. "Please don't put the part about me seeing a therapist in the article."

"I'll scratch it from the record."

I scribble notes as I often do in interviews. Mr. Cannon said, "Don't try writing everything down word for word. Abbreviate. Make the notes make sense to you. If you need to write something from your childhood that only makes sense to you, do it."

"I'm thirsty," I say. "I'm going to get a Mountain Dew."

I buy the biggest size they have. I'm thankful the cup is Styrofoam. I take a big gulp from my drink the second I get it.

We've only bowled three frames. Bowling is basically the side operation

If I break 100 any time I bowl, I'll be more than lucky.

I take another big gulp of my drink and set it by my feet. I remove the lid and take out a water bottle from my backpack.

"Nice," Avery says, blowing a puff of smoke my way. "Vodka?"

I nod.

"What do you want people to know the most about you? Or how do you feel the most misunderstood?"

"Those are two different questions. I'd want people to know that I'm a person too. I'm like them. I get hurt. I have feelings. I'm not just some freak. I feel like people think

I'm asking this big thing, that I want them to notice me when I only want to be treated like everyone else."

"Why run for Snow Coming King then?" I ask. "I mean you'll obviously draw attention to yourself."

"I want to be viewed as normal. It'll be like the school acknowledging me."

I look at Avery.

I'm silent, smoking my cigarette.

Avery looks at the ground. A small cue on lying or truth aversion.

"Okay ... there's more. Don't put this in your article though," Avery lets out a sigh. "Ben Benson came up to me and told me someone like me would never be popular enough to be Snow Coming King, and a person like me doesn't belong."

Tears fill the brims of Avery's eyes without falling down his face.

"He's a douchebag. Do you want to prove him wrong?"

Avery nods. "I want to prove everybody wrong. And why not vote for me?"

"Would it be safe to say you're running for Snow Coming King because you just want to be accepted?"

Avery nods. "People just don't understand either. They act like one day I got up and decided to *switch teams*. I don't feel like I had a choice in any of this. I've felt like this since elementary school. It goes beyond complete rational thought. I literally feel trapped in a body that isn't mine. A boy trapped in a female body. It made me depressed for a while. I debated killing myself. People said I was just a tomboy or that I'd feel different one day. In middle school, it only got stronger; I felt trapped inside the wrong body. Since the end of middle school, I decided to act like who I am and be myself."

I listen and write down more notes.

"Don't put the thing about me wanting to kill myself in the article either."

"I won't. Our interview is complete."

I can't help but ask, "How do you know Dustin?" It's interesting how people meet and become friends.

"He's one of the few friends who has been there for me since middle school. We fell out for a bit but reconnected. He never once asked me to be something I wasn't. He lives on the same block as me."

"I only remember him from middle school," I admit. "I don't really know him."

We smoke another cigarette, and the smoke fills the air.

I spot Carmen's tanned legs before I see her face and I put my cigarette out into the ash tray.

When she comes up to me, she wrinkles her nose. "Were you smoking?" she asks.

"No," I say.

She steps closer to me. Her nostrils flare. "You know smoking is the leading cause of death. It can cause lung cancer, and it's more addicting than every drug except heroin, right?"

"Of course."

She comes extra close to me, like she wants to kiss me or lick my face, which is weird.

"You're lying."

"No, I'm not."

"Yes, you were smoking. I thought our relationship was built on honesty."

"There's no relationship." It sounds harsher than I mean it to.

"She's already nagging you?" Avery asks.

"I guess so."

I turn to Carmen. "Besides, you're the one that got me started on smoking certain things."

"But it's a natural flower not altered by all of those nasty chemicals and has many positive effects. Reduced anxiety. Increased creativity. More relaxation."

"I know when you're bullshitting me."

"Smoking cigarettes is unattractive."

Dustin arrives and we all bowl together.

I bowl atrociously the first few frames.

Carmen gets a strike.

"That was pure luck."

Carmen smirks. "Thanks, congratulations!"

My ball goes in the gutter like some magnetic force attracts all of my balls there regardless of how straight I try to throw them. Athletic blood fails to run through my veins.

Carmen's next ball knocks down seven pins. She picks up the spare on the second throw.

"I hate you," I say.

"I'm sorry for your emasculating performance, but I can't help my dad took me bowling a decent amount as a kid. I think it was because they always had beer at the bowling alleys, and I was somewhat entertained."

My score is 48. Didn't even break 50. It's the lowest out of all four of us.

Before leaving, I get up to go to the bathroom.

Staring at the bathroom stalls, unkept and dirty, the profanity stands out the most. Holden Caulfield would be rolling in his grave. He would throw a fit at the words in here, as there's more than an F-bomb or two. In addition, there's copious colorful messages of other males inquiring about fellatio, talk of people's mothers, and random phone numbers who I doubt—or at least *hope*—nobody calls. But I'm not Holden, so I don't try to clean it up and if the people in charge of the facilities don't care enough to, I don't see why I should be the Good Samaritan and even try.

After all, I'm not a goddamn janitor.

We say good-bye and Carmen and I leave together even though we drove separate.

"What else are we going to do tonight?" Carmen asks.

"We?"

"Yes, us. It's still relatively early for a Friday night and I'd say we're reasonably young."

Chapter 34

We decide to go to Carmen's house after picking up snacks at Meijer. We don't go to the self-checkout lane; it's too inhumane.

"Eventually there'll only be self-checkout lanes in stores, and they won't even have humans working here. Robots will take inventory and stock all the shelves," I say.

"Okay Mr. Pessimistic."

Nobody's home when we arrive at Carmen's house.

"Where are the parental units?"

Her dad drinks heavily, and his whereabouts vary sporadically. As a child, she had to count his empty beer cans to know if she could ride home with him. The most she remembers counting is 11.

"My dad is at the bar, which one I don't know. And my stepmom I couldn't care less about."

Her stepmom and her rarely get along. Carmen will be nice to her, make food, and do chores. Her stepmother rarely makes dinner, but when she does, she'll rarely even make food for Carmen.

"Can we go in your room?"

"I don't think that's appropriate."

"Why not?"

"Because ..."

"Your reasoning is impeccable."

"I'm not easy."

I let out a sigh. "I know that.'"

"Good. I think maybe you'll think I'll want to do that weird shit we did when we were on shrooms."

I stare at the ground and am aware my face is red. However, I still feel oddly aroused at the same time, and I'm not sure what this says about me as a person.

"You made this awkward," I observe.

"It's what I do."

"I'm aware. I knew since the first time I saw your robotic walk."

She tries suppressing a smile but fails. "I'm teasing you anyway."

We relocate to the basement. The steps creak as we walk down.

We watch Carmen's favorite movie, *12 Monkeys*.

"The plot is so implausible," I say. Although any time travel movie runs into the same plot loop; each past event creates a ripple effect on the present, and it makes you think about chance. But changing the past alters the future and the same person can't exist twice at the same time.

"You have to get into it. It's a good movie. The *best* in fact."

"Highly improbable."

We continue watching.

I point out the biggest plot hole. "The whole virus thing not only bringing the world to a halt but killing everybody? That would never happen."

"It's a movie. It's made up. Jesus Christ."

"Leave my savior out of this."

"Oh my God, you are so annoying."

"I doubt you'd wanna be with anybody else right now. So I'm trapped with *you*."

She looks at me, arches an eyebrow and does this thing where she puts her lips together. "I think you're a willing captive."

We both sit Indian style. My hand kind of brushes her hand underneath our knees as we watch the movie. To my surprise, she grabs my hand and, like this, we're holding hands. She's so confusing sometimes. She likes me one second. The next she doesn't. I never know what I'll get with her.

"Do you know my mother told me once she wished she never had me," Carmen says.

It comes out of nowhere and it lays a thickness over the air.

"That's horrible." I break the silence.

"She meant it though. It's not like she tried to take it back all the way. She kind of did, but I could tell she meant it. That's why I chose to live with my father. Even though he's an alcoholic, he never once said he didn't want me."

Chapter 35

Right when I'm changing for Sports Skills this freshman, Ryan, grabs the locker next to me.

"Look at my back," he says. Nail marks stretch from his shoulder blade to his waist.

"I had sex with Teressa Goodwind," he says. She's a senior and I don't know her all that well. Except now, I guess I know during intercourse she scratches people worse than a cat. Sometimes I think every kid in this entire school is getting laid except me.

"It was so good. She left so many marks."

"Might want to make sure that doesn't get infected," I advise.

He seems over-enthusiastic. But I guess, again, if I was only a freshman and had my first taste of what sex was like, I'd feel a step above my peers. Back then, I only remember *talking* about sex and brainstorming/fantasizing possible improbable scenarios, which looking back only seems preposterously optimistic boarding on brainless fixations.

"Are you guys together?" I ask.

A confused look spreads across his face like he failed to put a label on their new-formed sexual bond. I almost wish I hadn't asked him, so he didn't need to think too hard about it. I mean *that* part I have experience with. All of it going downhill and not working out the way you imagined.

"I don't know," he says. "We just had sex this once, well, twice this weekend."

"How'd you meet?"

"She's just always been my neighbor, kind of like an older sister to me."

I remember when we first started the year. All of the juniors and seniors walked with more pep in their step as we watched the girl's gym class train at the same time.

"Looks like the fresh meat is in this year boys," somebody said.

A younger freshman said, "Why can't you go after girls your own age?"

"It's the rule of two years," someone else explained. "Girls always like older guys. The magic number is two grades. Each year freshmen tend to date more juniors than fellow freshmen."

I applaud Ryan for breaking this trend and scoring an older girl.

We shower after our workout.

This sophomore who looks more on the emo side, wears tight pants, and styles his hair in that emo fashion where it is long and sticks up in the back is the unexpected candidate to begin official post-shower Locker Room Talk.

"Are those girl pants?" Connor asks him. The tighter jeans made of super stretchy soft material compared to our rough jeans. We've all felt the material and *wished* they used it to make guy jeans as well, but nobody admits this.

"They are," Vince, the sophomore says. "They don't look like it, but they're actually more comfortable than guy jeans."

We give him strange looks.

Vince turns to Drew Carson—a good-looking but relatively quiet junior who I've never once heard engage in any of the Locker Room Talk—and says, "I went to a party this weekend. Man, pot makes chicks so horny. I had sex with this chick from Orchard View. Am I right? Have either of you been there?"

Vince looks at me as well.

"I've been there without the weed," Drew says, smiling.

Chapter 36

We occasionally have a drill where we have to pretend there is a bomb or the threat of a gunner in the school. This is where we exit the building in a straight line. Walking, not running, giving the shooter a perfect opportunity to take out each one of us with ease. (The administration fails to acknowledge this part, which makes no sense; at least if we were in the classrooms, the shooter would have to *walk* around to shoot all of us.)

The drill falls in the middle of Physics.

We walk single file. Carmen walks in front of me. She's not wearing a skirt today, but I wish she was. Instead, ripped jeans cling to her buttocks. Her purple sweater offers bagginess her jeans do not.

"I'm cold," she says.

"You do realize it's in the middle of *winter*," I say for about the third time.

"You've already said that like twenty times."

While other parts of the globe may experience T-shirt temperatures year-round, in Michigan it changes by the minute. One second it may be hot and the next cold, but the norm from November to February is snow and to be bundled up with boots, winter coats, sweaters, and thick socks. I fantasize about moving somewhere warmer, but I don't want it to be Florida because only old people move there, and I wouldn't last a month with those types of drivers.

"You should have dressed better."

"So cold." She shivers.

"This drill was planned a month ago."

"I forgot."

Looking at her shivering makes me realize I'd do anything to keep her warm.

"Take my coat."

"Oh, no, I couldn't." Even as she says this, I feel like it's a half-ass effort, and I know she will wear my coat.

"Such a true gentleman." She *knows* I hate being called a "gentleman."

"Chivalry is not dead yet, but you're close to killing it."

The irony is if somebody would actually bomb the school and it happened to be a student, they'd know the bomb drill and where we would go, and if they happened to be serious and possessed a functioning brain, they'd know to put the bomb in the church in the first place.

Carmen no longer shivers as we trot to the church, an imperial march, like an army. I remember the instructions in the letter given to us where I forged my father's signature. *The students will not disrespect the church in any way. No student is to touch anything in the church. Silence and respect is expected.*

I think about church versus state and how this is clearly a physical violation of it.

Next, I think about how one teacher said, "It's amazing. Cigarettes aren't allowed on school property, even if a student is 18, yet when they walk across the street these cigarettes magically appear."

Teachers are maybe not as dumb as they let on with such things, but nobody enforces certain rules. And as most of the people who go to the church know, The Administration's discipline is out of jurisdiction. It's only enforced when rare cases of vandalism occur—one time Principal Harris announced somebody smeared feces at the church and they would punish those responsible.

We walk along the sidewalk. As instructed by his superiors, Mr. West gave us clear instructions and said, "If anybody talks on the walk to the church, they will get a detention."

A little girl who can't be older than three sees all of us walking. "Hi!" she yells.

"Hi," Carmen says back with excitement.

I look back at Mr. West. He undoubtedly heard Carmen. He looks the other way as if he's failing to acknowledge hearing her.

We arrive at the church.

"Make sure not to touch anything. We are guests," Mr. Carter, the economics teacher waiting at the entrance, reminds us. Which I'd like to point out that our asses will touch the seats and our shoes will hit the floor and we're not supposed to talk during this drill. Mr. Carter is setting a poor example.

By the time we arrive, there are no seats and we are forced to sit on the floor.

Valerie, who I went to elementary school with—her dad's Jamaican and her mom's from Muskegon—sees me. "McCarthy!" she yells.

Again, this is a goddamn church and the noise *echoes* throughout the entire auditorium. To be honest, she is one of the few girls I still talk to, or who I have talked to this long (even though we really haven't started talking until freshman year when she sat in front of me during Geometry; she'd turn around in her seat and talk to me). Her skin is a perfect rich milky chocolate cream color. Her breasts jut out from her torso.

Even Chris, who sat next to me, said, "Dude, she has a nice rack," when she walked to the pencil sharpener.

"Valerie!" I yell, risking a detention. She comes over to me and hugs me.

"It's been so long."

"It's only been a couple of days."

"But still ... remember when we had Geometry together?"

"Of course."

"And we had Mr. Porter."

"Who could forget."

"Let's circumcise this triangle."

We both laugh. He'd say odd things to male students telling them their best work was done in the dark.

For a second, there's this silence.

"I was thinking about getting a haircut," I say. My bangs used to protrude as an overgrown mess from my forehead, impeding my vision at times. Now, I keep up on my haircuts slightly better.

"You can't get your hair cut," Valerie says. "I like when it's longer. Your hair just has to be in your eyes."

I smile.

By the time we leave the church, Carmen is stomping.

"What's wrong, princess?" I ask.

"Nothing, *your hair just has to be in your eyes.*"

"Are you jealous?"

She doesn't look at me or say anything.

"Just take your stupid coat." She shoves it at me and doesn't say a word—exactly like we're supposed to—the whole march back.

Chapter 37

My article received generally positive reviews from my peers. I'd say to my surprise, but I've yet to determine their standings on certain issues and completely predict their reactions. There seems to be a surprisingly genuine amount of support for Avery.

Mr. Cannon hands our grades back on our latest articles.

Jeanna lets out hysterics, almost bursting into tears. She raises her hand. "How come I got an F?"

"Remember at the beginning of the semester how I said anybody who spells somebody's name wrong gets an automatic F on the assignment?" Mr. Cannon replies.

He made it very clear. Spelling names wrong undermines anybody's journalistic integrity. If you can't even get that simple piece of information right, how can anybody else believe anything you wrote in your article? He clearly stated, "If I find out you spelled a name wrong in any of your articles it's an automatic F. If you're unsure of the spelling, you can simply ask the person to confirm it."

"But I was close."

"Close doesn't cut it in journalism." Mr. Cannon's facial expression doesn't even change.

"But—"

"No *buts* about it. You can get extra credit by finding errors in local printed papers."

If we notice any spelling errors—which Mr. Cannon assured us there were plenty in printed publications, especially *The Muskegon Chronicle*—we can get extra credit points by circling the mistake and bringing it in.

Jeanna slumps in her desk, tears form in her eyes.

Thankfully, I've yet to succumb to this error. The truth, of course, is Mr. Cannon knows he couldn't possibly find all of the errors in the spelling of people's names, but I get his point about being accurate.

"Article formats," Mr. Cannon begins today's assignment. "We've touched on this before, but I want to drive it home. There are many different formats. Hard news—your court cases, crime beats, and others—follows the inverted pyramid format. Place the most important pieces of information first allowing the reader to skim the article. Most people don't read the entire article."

He touched on this at the beginning of the year.

I rarely cover hard news, and Mr. Cannon admitted most of our articles won't be. After all, there aren't an abundance of shootings, burglaries, or court cases in school. The latter of which the administration would never allow us to write about in the first place.

"Our other articles allow more variety. Sports articles tend to stick to more of an inverted pyramid format but allow some leeway. Opinion pieces rarely follow this, and profile pieces don't either." Mr. Cannon pauses, "This is a review, not new information."

We get to work on an in-class assignment, writing a brief hard news piece on a plane crash. Mr. Cannon provides us with all of the details using a projector and a paragraph of information.

"Is this a real plane crash?" Blane asks.

"It's a fictional plane crash, but we're pretending it's real." There's all of the details along with a few quotes from air-traffic control, the company that owns the plane, bystander observations, and the Federal Aviation Administration's (FAA) official statement. According to the bible—which was a required purchase at the beginning of the semester: the Associated Press (AP) Stylebook—many abbreviations are used in journalism, but we identify the abbreviation the first time using it in an article. That's actually the book's title, *The Bible of the Newspaper Industry*. I'm not even kidding. Which suits me because I'd rather have this than the actual Bible.

Other topics the book covers are standards related to how to format dates, times, and proper ways to name things.

As Mr. Cannon walks by me, he says, "I think your last article struck a chord, Mr. McCarthy. Good work."

I write my assignment beginning with the basics. The who, what, where, when, and why.

On Saturday, February 11 at around 8:30am, an American Airline flight crashed near Boulder, Colorado. Thirty-six people have been reported dead, and the cause of the crash is still under investigation according to the National Transportation Safety Board (NTSB). The Federal Aviation Administration (FAA) says weather conditions may have been a factor.

Mr. Cannon always tells us he wants us to learn all about the rules of journalism, but then adds, "Know the rules, so you can break them."

Chapter 38

Mr. Hopper doesn't lecture us much about our imaginary country and our laws. Instead, he talks more about the upcoming job shadow project. "I expect ..."

I zone out as he goes over the assignment.

"I didn't know you were so into chicks without dicks," Benson whispers to me.

"Did you like my article?" I whisper back.

Benson's looking for a reaction. I've met people like him before and sometimes a non-response is the best response.

"Sure, let's just walk around promoting it."

"Promoting what? Another person?"

"A he/she?"

"Either way a he or a she is a person regardless if they chose to associate themselves as the opposite sex."

"You're what's wrong with America." He lets out an aggravated sigh.

"It's not our overly aggressive military policy, our sky-high obesity rates due to all of the processed food, or the lack of universal health care coverage?"

We are having a whispering argument under our breath.

He looks dumbfounded. "It's not natural."

"Is anything we do really natural? Being locked up for countless hours a day learning all this shit they think is important and being fed all of their lies?"

"You're just promoting it. Our school is going to be the laughingstock out of all the schools."

"I never thought I'd see the day when I got downcast for promoting equality."

Mr. Hopped shoots us a look. Our whisper argument may have exceeded the volume level of a whisper argument.

"Mr. Benson and Mr. McCarthy, do 15 push-ups each for interrupting when someone else is speaking," Mr. Hopper orders.

"I feel like I do more push-ups here than I do in Sports Skill," I mutter. Benson lets out a laugh.

Avery purposely runs into me outside of government class. "I've been getting a lot of attention," Avery says.

"Is that good or bad?" I ask.

"Mostly good," he says. "I've had a bunch of people say they would vote for me for Snow Coming King."

The next step in the process is each of us must write down two names for the vote. The vote will be conducted the week after Valentine's Day. The school will announce the candidates and the following week each of us will vote on the candidates. On whichever Friday it falls on, the Snow Coming Queen and King are announced.

I reluctantly sit at Benson's table in the lunchroom. Carmen and I don't have the same lunch. I don't have a typical table I frequent in the lunchroom. I'm not some loser sitting alone—unless by design and I'm studying (or assembling cheat sheets) last minute for a test I forgot about or whipping up an assignment—but I realize I'm not the most sought-after scholar to commiserate with. If it'd be a movie, I would eat in the bathroom stall, but I find that too unappetizing and unsanitary to even consider that a remote possibility.

Some days I pack lunch. Others I go out for lunch. Others it's whatever food the school cafeteria decides to fry up. Today's special: fried macaroni and cheese balls.

"It's like they'll just fry up any leftovers," I say, glancing around. I'm thankful I opted for Taco Bell and am exploring the heavenly goodness of a crunch wrap supreme. It's a true send from the gods: seasoned beef, with a crunchy shell, sour cream, lettuce, tomatoes, and cheese sauce all wrapped in a tortilla.

"I got pulled over the other day by an idiot cop," Benson says.

"What were you doing?" I ask.

"I was driving a little over the speed limit. The cop acted like he was making the biggest drug bust in history."

Benson does look like a typical stoner with his curly hair, slow speech, and slow movements. But the kid is straight edge. He doesn't drink or smoke at all.

"He held up a garbage bag in my trunk and was like, *what's this?* It was just a bag with nothing in it. He asked me ten times if I had been smoking pot."

I laugh.

Despite Benson being kind of an asshole and a general douche, he has funny moments. It makes me think of how maybe nobody is completely good or completely bad.

"I think if anyone could benefit from taking a few tokes of the bowl, it'd be you," I observe. "It might loosen you up a bit."

He scoffs. "I don't do drugs."

"It's a plant. It is *natural*. I guarantee you, you won't die. You'll learn to relax a bit and not be such a prick."

Which is true. I've noticed desirable changes in the attitudes of my peers. Some of the douchest assholes have mellowed out due to the ganja. However, of course, some of the people have become full-blown stoners with virtually no drive to do anything except smoke their next bowl, but there's no point in using this in the argument.

"Then I'll move in with grandma, live in her basement until I'm thirty, drop out of college, and sit around eating Cheetos all day," Benson says.

"I'd prefer Doritos. They're the superior chip for munchies."

"I'm so lucky I have an easy sixth hour."

"Which class?" I'm all about slack classes. "I have Women and Minorities."

"I work in the office. Half of the time they let us do our homework."

While I probably wouldn't be doing my homework, I get the importance of having "slack" classes during the day.

Avery stands next to the table.

Benson looks at him then looks down.

"Is it okay if I sit here?" Avery asks.

"Of course," I say.

"I wasn't talking to you." Avery looks at Benson.

Benson looks up. "Look, I'm sorry. I was an asshole the other day. I didn't mean it." He looks surprisingly serious.

"Such a change of heart," I interject.

"I was blowing off steam and I misdirected it towards Avery. I'm sorry. I really am."

Avery sits down.

"Let's not talk about it," Avery takes a bite of a lackluster sandwich and eyes it. "I need to get a job, so I don't need to eat this shit for lunch."

It occurs to me: Pops never made me get a job. He said as long as I was busy with the school paper, I didn't need to get one, but the second I stopped and had no extracurricular activities, I'd have to get a job. I always told him I wouldn't go to school unless he gave me gas money; I'm not going to literally *pay* to go to a place I hate.

"Doritos or Cheetos?" I ask.

"Huh?" Avery looks at me confused.

"The superior snack food," Benson clarifies. "We were debating this."

"Doritos obviously."

"How can you answer that quickly? While I understand Doritos have crunch, Cheetos are cheesier which is essential for any cheesy snack, the puffy non-crispiness, allows you to savor the cheese flavor longer."

Avery and I glance at each other.

"I'm gonna step down from this debate," I whisper.

"You make a valid argument," Avery says, laughing. "I don't feel like debating."

"So I win?" Benson asks, like he's surprised somebody let him get his way.

"Are you a middle child?" Avery asks.

"What is that supposed to mean?"

"Answer the question."

"Well ... yeah younger brother. Older sister, she already graduated."

"You're the middle child who is never right and goes unnoticed. That explains a lot."

Benson, agitated, says, "Both my parents love all of us equally."

"I'm sure it's a three-way tie," Avery says, smiling. "I'm a middle child too."

"Do you know what I am?" I ask.

"An only child." Benson and Avery say it simultaneously.

"Wait ... how do you know?"

They both start laughing.

Chapter 39

Even though Carmen and I were in the same class, we didn't talk at first. We only IMed. It was the whole paralyzing fear coursing through me that prevented me from ever talking to my first crush, Rachel Martin, in person. I got Carmen's AIM from Rita when she went to the bathroom. Rita asked, "Why do you want it?"

Finally, one time, I messaged, *Can we talk on the phone?*

Yes.

You have to be the one to pick up so I don't have to ask for you.

I'll be the one picking up.

I felt a flutter in my chest and my pulse beat quicken. Immediately, I wanted to back out. But I picked up the receiver and dialed the number. The whole time worried she wouldn't pick up.

"Hey," she said.

"Hey."

"You don't normally do this, do you?" she asked.

"Definitely not, but I want to."

"We talk *so* much on AIM. How come you never talk to me in class?"

"Because ... I don't know ... you're always so busy talking to your friends and I don't think you'd want to talk to me."

"Just walk up to me and start talking. Don't worry so much."

"Okay."

"I *want* you to talk to me."

Afterwards, I messaged her: *You have a sexy phone voice.*

Really? I always thought it was too deep for a girl's.

It's not. It's perfect.

The next day I walked up to her with a purpose and casually talked to her in front of her friends. Pretty soon this led to us talking in the hallways. Taking walks after school. And eventually: The Date.

Then the period of us not talking for a brief bit.

Early on when Carmen and I started talking in person, she asked, "Why me? I'm not that special."

"I don't know," I said, reluctantly. We were out by the football field, walking after school.

"There had to be something? You just started messaging me."

"I felt like I *had* to."

In Physics sometime in September last semester we had a few different people in the classroom. We had Ed Norris and Chase King. Mr. West left the room while we worked on labs.

Ed was overweight. As a result, the butt of many jokes, but he was always a nice kid. Never mean-spirited and despite years of bullying kept a cheerful disposition. King on the other hand enjoyed tormenting people. When people decided not to try out for soccer last year because they couldn't stand their over-conservative Bible-thumping douchebag couch, he'd openly yell "quitter" at them in the hall. He's the type of guy that trips his own teammates in practice to look better during a drill.

"Are you going to have two lunches today?" King asked Ed loudly.

Ed didn't respond.

"Too busy thinking about food?"

King went up to Ed's lab, which happened to be my lab. I admit I froze. I wish I could have done more.

"Are you going to eat your pain away?"

Finally, I had enough. "Dude, —"

"Just leave him alone, okay?" Carmen swooped in all of a sudden and was standing by us. "Does it fill some kind of sick twisted gratification in you bringing others down? He did nothing to you, literally nothing. But you want to be a bully and make him feel bad. Do you remember when you got picked on in elementary school for having braces? Did you like that? Did you like when kids called you 'metal mouth'?"

King looked at her "I—"

"You have no excuse. Apologize to him."

"How did you know that?" King asked.

"I know many things."

"I'm not going to—"

"Apologize now."

Carmen's eyes blazed with fury.

The whole class watched the scene unfold.

"I'm sorry," King said, sheepishly. Definitely *not* meaning it. He walked back to his lab.

Ever since then, I thought she was even more attractive, and I *had* to talk to this girl and learn more about her.

What I didn't say was Rita wasn't the first one to say I was gay. It started sometime in middle school. I don't remember the exact details, but it was a joke that got out of control.

Brandon Matthews was being made fun of. Kids were saying he was "queer."

One day, I said, "Maybe I'm gay too. Who wants to be gay with me?"

The kids looked at me strangely but laughed. I kept adding to this gag, and I noticed they picked less and less on Brandon.

I enjoyed making my peers laugh.

By the time I got to high school I realized it followed me. People would say it when they weren't around me. I heard about whisperings at parties where my name would come up, and somebody would ask, "Isn't that kid gay?"

Talk about killing my chances with the girls before I even started. I dropped the routine.

I'm not saying there's anything *wrong* with being gay, but as someone fully interested in girls, it kind of interfered with what I was going for.

That's why when Carmen told me Rita asked if I was gay, it upset me.

Sometimes when I think about Avery, I think he has a chance to tell his story too. If it will take away from my peers saying stuff like this, I think it's worth intervening.

Chapter 40

In Michigan to say, "It snows," would be the biggest understatement of the 21st century. I mean it *snows*. Back in the 70's, my dad remembers the snow piling up so high people couldn't see out of their living room windows, let alone open their doors. While we have yet to reach this monumental amount again, it's safe to say once it snows and sticks it will keep snowing and unless you like winter sports—which I detest—you will be stuck inside for the next eight months.

Today the snowflakes fall down in a whirlwind and there's no end in sight. I've been up for about an hour and am patiently watching the T.V. listings on the news as the school closings stream at the bottom in alphabetical order.

It starts with Allegan High School, goes to all these other ones. By the time it gets to "G" my heart skips a beat, and when it's on "K" I'm at full alert. Kentwood Schools Closed. Klarksdale County Schools Closed. Kramer County Schools Two Hour Delay.

Larsen School District Closed.

They could have made a mistake?

Maddison County Schools Closed, Mason County Schools Closed. Montgomery County Schools Two Hour Delay. Portage schools closed.

The thing about Lakewood High is they *hate* cancelling school. Other schools will have three inches of snow and cancel but here we could have *three feet* of snow and school would still be on—there was one time we had over a foot of snow and we still had to go to school. Today we already have six inches on the ground with six more expected to fall.

Carmen calls me and asks for a ride to school. While this is atypical, it's not completely unusual. Sometimes her stepmom steals her car. Even though it's out of my way, I oblige.

The worst part about driving in the snow is my tires spin. I slide all over the place. This happens to also be the best part of the ride.

"I risked my life coming to get you," I say when she opens my passenger door.

"Somebody is over-exaggerating."

"The things I do for you."

"You're such a sweetheart."

Her knee pushes into mine, and I swear she does this shit on purpose sometimes.

"You're so quiet. What are you thinking about?" She stares at me.

I move my knee.

Even with the windshield wipers on, the snow obstructs my vision. As we always say in Michigan, it's amazing how many old drivers end up in the ditch the first snowfall each year. It's like 40-year-olds completely forget how to drive.

"We never have a friggen snow day," I say.

"What's your favorite thing about me?" Carmen asks out of nowhere.

"Probably how annoying you are or the fact that you never shut up and always keep talking."

She punches my arm.

"Hey, I'm driving. I'm being a responsible young man with my eyes on the road."

"Really? Are you?"

"Is somebody fishing for compliments?"

"Tell me."

"I like that you keep talking and there's rarely a dull moment." I like that we can talk for hours literally and never run out of things to say to each other. This is unusual for me. Generally, if you put only guys in the same vicinity, we will talk a bit but after a while the conversation lulls. (This is especially true at the beginning of the day before first hour.)

"I mean physically."

"Probably your eyes." Sometimes they look more like Sapphire blue. Other times closer to Azul blue, depending on the lighting. They hold a world of depth and many mysteries I doubt I will ever solve.

"What else?" she leans into me.

"Is this supposed to be Shower Carmen with Compliments Day?"

"You used to say a lot more." This is true. All the AIM conversations. All the pictures she sent me. I have them saved on the desktop at home.

"Things changed."

"But what else?"

"I like your legs." She has the legs of a goddess, she really does. Tanned and smooth and you just want to run your hands all over them and it's easy to think about other stuff as well, but I will not go into locker-room detail.

"Yeah?" She looks at me.

"Don't look at me like that."

"Like what?" She gives me pouty lips. Her lips are full and very kissable.

"My turn. What do you like about me?"

"Your ocean blue eyes," she says. "They're green and blue, and if you look at them just right, they look like Lake Michigan on a calm day."

"What else?" I don't miss a beat.

"You're really smart and a good writer and journalist."

When I zoom into the parking lot, almost late, I cut across the lines, which is a big no-no. Before I even exit my vehicle, the Parking Lot Nazi (also known as Mr. Guerrez) pulls up by my car. "Cutting across the lines is not allowed," he scowls.

"My bad."

He hands me a ticket and our dialogue is complete.

Carmen is quiet as we walk in for a second. "He could have at least let you go with a warning."

"They're trying to toughen us up for the *real world*." I use hand quotations around the last two words.

Carmen snorts.

"And the only way we'll ever get a snow day is if we make one."

"There's an idea."

Chapter 41

There's this tradition at Lakewood High, where each time a week or so before Valentine's Day we can purchase these big suckers for a person. The money goes to whatever charity they choose at the time. We can write a brief message on them. And we can choose whether to put our name on it or not.

I'm watching Connor and some of the other guys trying to sell them in the lunchroom, going from table to table.

A group of freshmen are sitting on the far end of our long table.

"Buy one of our suckers for Valentine's Day," Connor says. "It's a sure way to get your girlfriend to blow you."

"I'd be careful of false advertising," I say, loudly, so all of the freshmen can hear me.

Connor looks smugly at me. "Want to buy one for Carmen?"

"I'll buy one since it does help animals in need." This time it's going to Heaven Can Wait. A non-kill shelter for animals.

Connor looks at me. "I wonder what message you'll write."

I contemplate this thought and try to think of what words I want. Obviously, he's right: I'm sending the sucker to Carmen. For a second, I hate myself and know it won't change anything between us. And it's not like she's my girlfriend so in a way it's probably a weak move on my part, but nevertheless, I decide to send her one.

I write my message, *You still walk like a robot.*

"Remember it's a personal message," I say when I hand Connor the paper.

I think about sending one to Valerie because it will doubtless make Carmen jealous if she finds out, but I'm not much of a plotter. Nor am I looking to cause a problem.

I chomp on my Little Caesar breadsticks—it's dollar breadstick day. Last year, the school decided to take away off-campus lunches. Little Caesar decided to bribe the school by buying a whole new computer lab. Of course, it wasn't officially a bribe. Only a generous donation. The result: we are now allowed to go off-campus again for lunch.

For another split second, I picture somebody else sending Carmen a sucker for Valentine's Day or her getting a plethora delivered to her desk. Mine not even standing out. My stomach tightens. But then I think it'd be worse if she only got two, say one from Luke Hansen and one from me. Direct competition.

I hate myself for thinking about it or even caring.

I debate buying another sucker and saying something else. I wish these types of things were simpler. If Carmen was my girlfriend—like I originally wanted—it'd all be so much easier. It's weird thinking maybe that timeframe passed. What went wrong?

Perhaps more sleuthing would have helped uncover the mystery of Carmen. Or she's a mystery I will never truly solve …

Chapter 42

Every year the usual suspects emerge when it comes to either homecoming or Snow Coming. Our elite popular group. The groups provide general fluidity—for example, how did Emily Hartman start hanging out with the "popular" crowd? Was it because she starting talking more to them and wanted to be in their little circle or because they picked her? Honestly, it seems like the first.

This left the usual subjects for Queen: Sarah Moore. Stephanie Taylor. Amelia Davis.

For King the general names emerge: Bret Ellen. Jimmy Reese. Dan Garrison.

Every school has them. The kids who are more liked, who seem to have this natural stroke of luck where everything they touch turns into this magical force.

These are the names everybody expects to pop up when we talk about Homecoming King and Queen or Snow Coming King and Queen.

One time Stephanie tried being nice and get everybody to vote for Sam. Stereotypically speaking, Sam isn't exactly the type of girl people would vote for as Snow Coming Queen. She's overweight, covered in freckles, generally pretty shy, and to be quite honest not all that physically attractive and doesn't have many friends.

This year—similar to the Sam year—there's this buzz in the air about Avery. My article made a difference. Or at least Avery is an option to consider.

Again, to say the peer groups are entirely stagnate at Lakewood High would be a lie.

"I know you're not a fan, Mr. McCarthy, but it's time for students to cast their nominations for the Snow Coming King and Queen," Mr. Hopper says. He hands out papers. Each student gets to write down one nomination for each.

"For some reason, I think you're going to participate in this one," Benson says.

"Just doing my civic duty."

I write down Avery for Snow Coming King, and I falter when deciding who to write down for the queen. In a way, I want to write down Carmen's name because I know she's undoubtedly the most beautiful girl at Lakewood High. But she's not the normal type of person people would write down. Sure, most guys would at least *admit* she's attractive, but similar to me, she's never exactly brought in the masses due to her popularity.

I write her name down anyway.

Chapter 43

"What was it like growing up in a neighborhood?" Carmen asks me.

This question comes out of nowhere. We're sitting in the school library, our feet barely touching, facing each other on the floor in the middle of the non-fiction section.

"I don't know how to answer that."

"I never grew up in one. All I remember was my dad getting drunk every night and my mom and dad fighting and throwing things ... I just want to know what it was like."

"It wasn't that great."

Even as I say it, I know it's a lie. To be honest, my childhood was the best part of my life—from the lack of social and mental awareness to the lack of awkwardness (or even understanding awkward moments), to everything being this big adventure, there was this hope for the future—and I'm aware it may never go back to how it was then. Even though as a child, I imagined this amazing life of driving around in a convertible, being able to go anywhere, listening to music.

"You're lying. You're a bad liar, which I guess is a good thing, but sometimes I feel like my entire life is a lie so ..."

I think of all the times she appears jovial in public, so animate with her hand gestures and facial expressions—yet I know there's this sadness creeping deep inside her, a melancholy she refuses to let the world see.

"I remember playing Pogs with my neighbors, playing capture the flag. The whole neighborhood would join. We played soccer. We played football. We had water gun fights."

"I'll have to vicariously live through you."

"It's childhood. It doesn't mean anything."

Friends forget each other. It turns out friendships formed in the yard playing football or capture the flag don't equate to real world friendships when you get older. If you put all of us miraculously in a room somehow, I doubt we'd even converse much aside from necessary pleasantries we mimic from adults.

"It shapes your whole life," Carmen says. "Certain people's childhoods really messed them up and they don't even know what a healthy relationship looks like."

Carmen's foot nudges mine.

I try to change topics. "If you could have any superpower, what would it be?"

"I don't know."

"I'd want tele-transportation. I could go anywhere in an instant."

Carmen's quiet.

"You could fly," I suggest. "Or you could have the power of invisibility."

"I think I had that superpower with both of my parents my whole life."

Chapter 44

Gramps is sitting in his usual recliner when we arrive. He's watching golf. While I don't mind watching sports, golf has to be the most boring sport in existence to watch on T.V. The guy hits a ball. You have to literally watch him walk for five minutes to get to the ball and then wait another five as he prepares his shot. Watching T.V. can't get any worse than this. Sports can't get any worse than this.

I used to go golfing with Gramps when I was about nine. We'd go to par threes. I never liked it *even* then, I just knew if I didn't go, he'd go alone, so I didn't want him to be lonely.

I hope when I'm old I'll never watch golf in a recliner.

When I'm older, I'm going to develop Selective Alzheimer's. I'm going to simply ignore everybody I have no desire to talk to by pretending I have no goddamn idea who they are.

Pops mentions my article in the school paper about Avery to Gramps. Despite showing relatively little interest in most of my life, Pops does always read the paper and my articles. I'm not sure if it's out of an obligatory sense to me or if he wants to keep up to date on school news.

"Check out the new article," Pops hands the paper to my grandpa, which is weird considering he didn't say anything to me about it. He rarely says much about anything involving the school paper.

My grandfather reads the paper in relative silence.

"That's part of the problem," Gramps snorts. "It's these kids are all confused by society and it's having a bad influence on them. We have to go back to how things used to be."

"Like segregation? Black people drink from this fountain. Whites over here. Public lynching?" I can't help myself.

"Today these kids are given too much freedom. They're being influenced by too much."

"There've always been gay people. Even back in your day. They just hid behind bushes."

"They were ashamed because they knew it was wrong. They made the *choice* to behave like that and now it's just supposed to be okay."

"Are you saying people choose to be gay?" I think a lot of behavior comes down to *both* nature and nurture. For example, nobody grows up knowing they want to smoke blunts every day or drink fifths of vodka, but then again, it's not like somebody is being shown they want to perform gay sex unless they're being sodomized as a child. Plus, I know this one kid, Brandon Mathews, from elementary school. I don't want to say you can figure out a person's sexual orientation from this age, but let's say when rumors started surfacing he was batting for the other team, none of us were exactly surprised.

"Well, they had to learn it from somewhere."

The dinosaurs all died out. Maybe this isn't a bad thing. They'll all die out again. The dinosaurs everywhere will die out, become extinct.

Eventually when my grandfather's generation dies out, the world will be a better place.

"I need to go for a walk," I get up and rush out of the door. For a second, I'm proud of myself for practicing restraint—another part wants to argue with my grandpa, but he's more than likely to die before he *changes*.

"Soon enough they'll let anybody switch from being a woman to a man ..." Those are the last words I hear as I take a stroll around the lovely neighborhood in sub-zero degree weather.

I know there's all this talk about climate change, but I wish we got it more in Michigan. I could use even a *slight* increase in temperature, and I'm willing to sacrifice a couple of glaciers just so I don't freeze to death.

People who complain about climate change have obviously never been to Michigan. Each year we get about ten cold months and two good months out of the entire damn year. Warmer weather sounds good.

I stroll until my cheeks are numb. Anything to avoid spending more time than necessary with gramps. I know we only see him for dinner probably once a month, but sometimes I wish he would be like all of the other grandparents in this state and move to Florida.

One of the last times Gramps gave me a ride home, he wasn't all with it. It's not that I think he was *trying* to drive shitty, but he just was. It was at night. He appeared confused by the street signs. He almost hit three mailboxes on the drive back.

In his defense, he noticed he was swerving.

"Bet I almost scared you there," he said.

"Yeah."

He came close to clearing a whole row of mailboxes without even noticing.

"I can't see as well as I used to, especially at night."

This was obvious. I could see how old people "accidentally" run into a marketplace full of children and kill a few people.

Safe to say, I never rode with Gramps again after this.

I'd only go with him if he let me drive.

When we pulled in, he said, "If I ever get too bad, you just have to take my damn license." He almost whispered it.

"I'm sure you'll be good for a few more years" I don't even know why I said it.

"Can you do me a favor?"

"What?"

"Don't tell your father about this."

"I won't."

"I'm not going to get to the point where I'm that old geezer running over ten people in a marketplace. If you ever think I am, then take away my license."

Later we watch a hockey game.

A Black goalie is playing for the other team. "I can't believe they let a Black guy play in the NHL."

You'd think it'd be like Jackie Robinson breaking the color barrier all over again.

"What do you mean they 'let him'?" my dad asks.

Gramps seems taken back by this. "They just let him play."

"He earned his spot like all of the other players earned their spot."

Just when you think your Pops can't surprise you, he somehow does.

Chapter 45

"It's amazing," Mr. Hopper says, pausing. "How some students return from lunch smelling like marijuana and can't even walk straight down the halls."

He shoots a few of us looks, although I rarely blaze during lunch break. I'm a dedicated student. A scholar as well as a gentleman.

"Today, we're going to talk more about checks and balances," Mr. Hopper says. "Can some of you name some of the checks and balances?"

Somebody mentioned how the president has the power to veto a congressional vote. Another points out that he can pardon anybody he pleases—including child-molesters and murderers. He talks about the whole thing and goes into more detail than anybody deems necessary.

I raise my hand.

"Yes, Mr. McCarthy?"

"I have one more. Newspapers are the fourth check on government. They can print anything they want because of freedom of the press and expose any of the corruptions of our government."

The class looks at me.

"Ehh," Mr. Hopper says. "While I get what you're saying, the newspaper isn't a part of government."

"But you said *checks on government*," I point out.

"The newspaper is not a part of government."

"Which is why they are the perfect ones to perform checks on it."

"I don't think you seem to understand—" Mr. Hopper is cut out by the announcement, the one we've been anticipating.

"We'd like to announce the winners of Snow Coming King and Queen," Principal Harris says. The guy is a joke over the loudspeaker. One time he talked to us about harassment, except he kept pronouncing it *hair-as-mint*, which only resulted in our laughter each time he said the word—taking away any value from what he actually intended us to get out of his spiel.

Principal Harris coughs into the microphone. "Sorry," he says. "The winner is Sarah Moore for Snow Coming Queen and Bret Ellen for Snow Coming King. Please congratulate our winners."

There's no friggen way.

"Looks like you didn't get the results you wanted," Benson snickers.

Chapter 46

Carmen's at my locker, waiting after school, looking around. An unsuspecting surprise.

"What do I owe this pleasure to?"

"We have to do something," Carmen says, frantically.

"What do you mean?"

"Something's wrong here. We know that Avery should have won."

"There's nothing we can do. It's a done deal."

"Something's fishy."

"How do you know that?"

"Think about it. Maybe call it a woman's intuition."

I shrug my shoulders. "Even if you're right I don't see what can be done ..."

We walk to Carmen's locker.

"Where is the investigative journalist in you? Remember how you told me about the guys who opened the bar in Chicago just to listen in on politicians, or how the one newspaper printed the articles on wiretapping even though the president told them not to? Or the one time you wrote about the soccer coach and how he forced his teammates to pray at dinner and made them run laps? Or how you wrote about politics in sports?"

Carmen's speaking quicker than usual.

"I'm surprised you remember any of that. But I think this is different."

"There is tampering here and an injustice. When have you stood down from any of that before?"

"Plenty of times."

"We have to do something." Carmen's eyes bead into me as I shovel books into my backpack.

"Did any of my articles change anything, actually?" It's a sad truth I don't like to linger on, but it's true, nonetheless. Politics in sports remains at large. I bet Coach Albert still forces the Muslims on his team to pray to his Christian god.

"But it lets people know what's happening."

"We don't even know if anything happened ... Maybe everyone just *said* they were going to vote for Avery and decided to vote for Bret Ellen instead."

People *say* things a lot, but the following through is not always there. Ask Carmen about what she said before our first date. I push this thought away.

"We can at least try to look into it."

"By *we* do you mean you want *me* to look into it?"

"No, I actually mean *we*."

"Because we make such a splendid team."

"We actually do." She grabs my arm, which is unlike her, but if I said I could predict anything this girl does that would be a complete lie.

Chapter 47

Carmen and I meet at Applebee's. Nothing fancy.

"Smoking or non-smoking?" the hostess asks us.

"Non-smoking," Carmen says quickly before I can get a word in.

When we're seated in our booth, I explain, "It's not like I smoke all the time, you know. When the circumstances call for it."

Carmen gives me a weird look I fail to decipher, but, if pressed, I'd label as a mix between amused and mischievous.

The waitress comes to take our order.

"I'll have a Coke with grenadine, please," I say.

"I'll have a water," Carmen says.

"Really? It's literally the most boring beverage invented. No flavor."

"Pop isn't good for you."

"Life isn't good for you."

"Okay, Mr. Cynical, let's get down to business."

I spot Connor and guys from Sports Skills sitting in a booth a ways away from us. All of them are laughing stupidly. I realize it probably appears to my overly sexual driven peers that I'm on a date with Carmen, which definitely isn't the case.

I hope they don't see me.

"Alright, we need to figure out what to do. There's absolutely no friggen way that Bret Ellen won."

"We don't know that." Even as I say it, I know it's not true.

"I talked to Elizabeth who works in the office, and she helped count the votes herself ... but she only started to count the votes and didn't get a full vote. She said she's not supposed to talk about it."

"It's her word against the administration."

"Write an article about it," Carmen says.

"I don't think the administration will think it's a good idea."

"You can do it."

Connor and his associates approach our booth on their way out. "Going to get lucky tonight, McCarthy?"

"It's strictly business."

"The business of getting some."

"There is a young woman present here. She doesn't need to hear your vulgarities."

"So you'll choke again like before?" I smell the vodka on his breath and realized they must be drunk.

"Maybe he won't." Carmen says. Sounding 100% serious and maintaining eye contact.

"Thatta boy!"

He claps me on the shoulder.

When they leave, I glare at Carmen. "Great. Now they'll inquire about all the sexual encounters that didn't happen."

"I had to stick up for your reputation, even if now it'll probably mean they'll gossip about me. Besides, I had to reassert your heterosexuality."

I snort.

"We have to do *something*," Carmen repeats for the fourth time. When she gets something on her mind, she never drops it.

We are smoking a bowl in my room. Pops is on another date tonight. Apparently, with a different woman because the first one didn't go so well. He kept the details of it vague, but I gathered she didn't want to see him again.

"I don't think there's anything we can do," I say. "Besides, I can't afford to get into any more trouble. Do you have any idea how many times I got called down to Gensen's office?"

"You like seeing his cowboy boots."

"I think he'd love to have an excuse to suspend me."

"You're a journalist. You're supposed to find facts. There's no way those election results were even close to accurate."

"Perhaps somebody tampered with it."

"So find out."

"I don't think it's worth messing with . . ."

I cough as I take another pull. The effects already have taken place. My mind races.

"It's the right thing to do."

"I don't think anybody cares about what the right thing to do is."

"You care about what the right thing to do is. You act like you don't, but I know deep down you do. I can tell."

Carmen has a meticulous sense of the pursuit of justice when she's high.

"Why don't you do it if you care so much?" I inquire.

"You're better at this than me. Exploring facts. You're a better writer than me."

Something she's never said before.

I'm silent for a second, basking in the new compliment. Carmen hates when people are better than her at anything.

Chapter 48

I dread Locker Room Talk during Sports Skills more than I usually do.

Sure enough, Connor smirks at me.

"How'd your weekend go?"

"Good." I keep my voice neutral.

"You're persistent, aren't you?"

"Don't know what you mean."

"You won't take no for an answer," Connor looks around, eagerly filling the others in. "So I saw this kid at Applebee's with Carmen. They were on a date."

"Not a date," I chime in quickly.

"She hinted that some activities might take place." Connor is laughing as the others are now too.

I feel my face grow hot.

"Nothing happened."

"It's okay. We won't tell anybody," Connor says. All of a sudden Locker Room Talk apparently carries some kind of confidentiality clause.

"Really, nothing happened."

"Don't want to kiss and tell?"

"We haven't done anything at all."

And even if I did, I wouldn't let it just be a moment for Connor to smirk, talk to others about, and spread rumors.

"Carmen isn't like that."

"She does have dick-sucking lips. Tell me those didn't feel good."

While I admit to noticing the voluptuous nature of her lips and having similar thoughts—sometimes provoked by Carmen herself—I don't want to talk about it with Connor.

"I mean feel free to send her my way."

The guys around him laugh.

I push him into the locker.

"What the—?"

"Quit talking about her."

"Something did happen?"

"No." I say it quickly and it sounds like a lie.

The locker room is hushed, and we carry on getting ready.

Before I head out, Connor says, "And if she isn't putting out, McCarthy, find someone who will. There are so many other hot girls in this school. Why waste your time settling on her? She's not that special."

There are tons of other attractive girls around. For example, Laura Hempkin. She developed into a beautiful girl and is always laughing and seems nice. But, the truth is when I like someone, really like someone, I tend to develop this stupid crush that lasts an eternity.

If we'd retrace the origin to my first crush, it developed in fourth grade. Rachel Martin. She had dark brown hair, more black than brown. Blue eyes. It was an irrational crush that didn't make sense. It lasted from fourth grade until ninth grade.

Now my latest crush is Carmen. Sometimes I wish I didn't like her as much as I do, but I can't control it. I'm drawn to her.

Out of six and a half billion people on this planet, I choose Carmen. Even though I know I could have been born someplace else and never met her. No matter how much I don't want to admit it, I'm glad I met her.

Chapter 49

Lily Mathews sits near Alex and me in Women and Minorities. She has cystic fibrosis. She revealed this in an article recently published. Unfortunately, I didn't get the honor of writing it. Marcie Erins did for her profile piece.

"Hey, how's it going?" she asks.

"Hey, good."

She has cute freckles on her nose. I remember looking up her jean skirt in middle school and her pink underwear. She works at Applebee's.

This makes me think of Rachel Martin. We had seventh grade English together. Mrs. Thomas, our teacher, turned on the news when the planes hit the twin towers on 9/11. She said, "This will go down in history, like Kennedy's assassination. You will always remember where you were on this day." I'll always remember on the morning of 9/11 I was in English class trying to catch glimpses up Rachel Martin's skirt. (She sat properly, and I was only successful on one occasion. Her underwear were blue.)

I remember Lily's constant coughing fits in middle school. She was diagnosed with CF when she was two but kept it relatively quiet; when the article came out, it was news to me.

Alex sits down next to me.

"The owner of Applebee's cried when she found out I had CF," Lily says. "I told her don't feel bad because then I'll start to feel bad. The doctors said I'd only live until fourteen. I got two extra years."

Here I am worried about Carmen and me not working out, wishing I wasn't alive, and all Lily is thinking is she got two extra years. It makes me feel ungrateful. It's weird thinking about how we know there is this bright future ahead of us where we will go to college, get married, and have kids and Lily won't get to experience any of that.

"I mean sometimes I don't even see the point in going to college when I know I don't have much longer to live."

"You're going to live to be 100," Alex says, but he doesn't convince any of us.

"Today we're going to talk about mascots," Mr. Gardner says.

Oh, joy.

"Some of them can be offensive," he says, pausing as if expecting us to provide input.

The class remains quiet.

"Can you think of any examples?"

The class remains quiet.

"Teams like the Washington Redskins, Kansas City Chiefs, Chicago Blackhawks, Cleveland Braves."

We remain quiet. Finally, I speak up, "Isn't it a sign of honoring and remembering their heritage?"

"No, it can seem like they're being made fun of with stereotypical costumes portraying Native Americans as *barbaric*."

Shannon speaks up. "Have you heard about the Native American team that named their team the Fighting Whities?"

We laugh.

"But it's not funny. It's serious," Mr. Gardner says, not even cracking a smile. "We need to break the stereotype."

"Do you think our school symbol might offend sailors?" I ask.

Mr. Gardner looks at me weird.

"That's a profession," he says. "Not a race. Something someone has no control over."

"What if they didn't have a choice and got into the job to please their parents?" I ask. I swear my dad thinks I'm going to be a goddamn accountant or work in a bank like him.

Mr. Gardner turns back to the board. "Anyway, there have been campaigns to change the mascots to something less offensive. I have an assignment for you," Mr. Gardner says. "I want you to pair up in groups of threes or fours and make a short story for children that in some way explores something we talked about in class so far. Not just today but any concept. We're going to read them to elementary school students."

The class lets out an audible sigh. Even though it should be noted this is one of the few actual assignments he's given us all semester.

Chapter 50

I pick up the phone. I hear a muffled voice and what sounds like somebody attempting to say my first name through sobs.

I recognize Carmen's voice.

"What's up?" She never uses my first name unless she's serious or upset.

"He …" She starts sobbing. A bunch of incoherent phrases follow.

"I can't understand you."

"Come here."

"Now? It's ten o'clock on a school night. Any reasonable gentleman would be in bed."

There's silence on the other end. She doesn't even scoff at my joke. I hear muffled crying. "Just come here, okay."

While I don't advise making the excursion across Seaway into the heights at night or anytime when it's dark, sometimes desperate times call for desperate measures. If I get shot, I will get shot. I make sure to wear neutral gang colors, avoiding red or blue. The urgency in Carmen's voice pushes me forward and I speed to her house.

When I arrive, I knock on the door. Carmen looks down and grabs my arm, leading me to the back.

"I hate my life."

"What happened?"

"He …" she starts crying and I move forward to hug her. I hold her.

"He was drunk and …"

More sobbing. While I always knew this was a part of Carmen's life, she's done a meticulous job of hiding it from me. Like she'll occasionally mention things, messed up things, but I haven't seen it first-hand.

"Tell me what happened."

She looks down. "He puked all over my clothes. My clean clothes I just washed."

I don't even need to ask who.

"Clothes can be re-washed." Although, I must admit, I'm unfamiliar with how this is done. I can only assume you throw your clothes in a pile on the floor and by some magic force they get cleaned. Perhaps elves come and do them when I'm sleeping or other sorcery takes place.

"It's not that, how he talks to me." She takes a deep breath. "I was out with Alexis. Hanging out. Talking. Not even drinking or doing anything bad. Not smoking pot. And when I get back, he's like *where have you been?* Like I'm some kind of slut."

She starts sobbing.

"We both know you're not."

She looks up at me, her mascara starts to drip down her cheeks, her face a complete beautiful mess of imperfection, and says, "But I wish he did."

And for this I have no words. I hold her and we don't talk for a bit. I wish I could absorb all of her pain and completely vanquish it.

Chapter 51

What happened between Carmen and I? It's the question everybody's curious about. People ask in round-about ways and straight forward ways. Even my dad, who met her—and he never asks me anything about girls—asked me. The truth is I don't exactly know what happened or how everything went awry.

All I know is you can talk to somebody every day for hours, gaining every piece of information. Share your deepest and darkest secrets and fantasies only to be told you're just a friend.

What happened is we went on a date. Don't think I'm the type of guy who obsesses over a girl just because we went on one date; it was more than that. We talked for months before this. Building each other up. Sharing everything.

Her dad set her up on her first date with someone's son from church. This is when he started to try to get sober and go to church before he inevitably returned to beer like he always does. Both of us were upset about the date. *I thought my first date would be with you*, I said. *Me too*, she said.

I learned she does her own laundry and knows how to make coffee. Her favorite color is sky blue but can change depending on her mood—which changes frequently.

She's told me stories I've tried to push into the back of my subconscious. Admitted to being afraid to fall asleep at parties. Being forced practically to sleep in the same bed as a guy. Nothing happened. He was in his boxers and she said he tried, but nothing happened. But she wouldn't mind seeing him again. I never even asked her who she was talking about, but knew it was a guy from a neighboring school. And it's not like I *know* those kids or want to, honestly.

I drove to her house, across Seaway, into the heights in a sketchy neighborhood. Her house was small with blue chipped paint and a rundown roof.

I walked up the door expecting her dad to meet me with a shotgun. To tell me to leave and never come back.

Her dad had an over-sized belly and a regular T-shirt on. "I'm here for Carmen."

"Come in."

He shook my hand. His grip was surprisingly soft. He was watching the Lions game on T.V. "The Lions are always losing," he said.

"Just like Lakewood High."

He laughed.

She came out of her room.

"Have her home by 9," he said. "Since it is Sunday."

When we pulled out of the driveway, Carmen said, "He hides his beer cans by the window, so a new person doesn't see them. My dad doesn't care if you have me home by 9. He'll be passed out by then anyway."

When we exited the car, she told me, "I like this. My favorite season is fall." Leaves decorated the ground and the warmth still lingered in the air.

We decided on a movie, *Something Like Heaven*. She wore a shirt with her shoulders exposed and I could see her purple bra.

"This movie is kind of lame," I said. A stupid movie about a ghost on her way to a blind date.

"I agree."

Afterwards we went back to my place. I introduced her to my dad.

We talked for hours. She tried picking up Winona, but she squirmed. "She's just an asshole," I said.

"The first time I got high was when I decided to join track freshman year. I remember walking around Meijers and liking everything pink."

"I would try it if I had the opportunity but never have."

"That's what it was like for me."

We said we'd do homework. We laid our books out on the bed. She drew circular flowers with a blue pen in a notebook.

"You don't seem very productive," I said.

Our knees touched. Her knee warm on mine. For a second, I thought it was incidental, immediately expecting her to pull away. But she kept her knee pressed onto mine. Not an accident.

And I felt it. Magnetic. Magic.

"What are you thinking?" she asked.

"Nothing," I said. I wanted to be as physically close to her as possible and not just because I wanted sex. I wanted more than that. To feel her entire warmth.

For every action there is an equal and opposite reaction.

"You're lying," she said, smirking. Of course, afterwards we talked about all kinds of things we'd like to do together but via AIM.

I dropped her off and walked her to the door and we hugged. In retrospect, I probably should have gone in for a kiss. But I thought this would be one of many dates.

"You guys had a lot to talk about," Pops said after I got back. "I questioned if it'd be as much as it was online."

I wondered if he heard some of the pot convos. Next, I wondered how much he analyzed my first date as I noticed his lack of dating.

And I still felt the warmth from Carmen's knee long after she left.

Later, the next week, she AIMed me, *I don't think I can do this. These just aren't relationship feelings.*

What do you mean?

I don't want a relationship right now. I just can't.

She was distant with me and barely talked to me beyond the superficial and took forever to respond.

Finally, I confronted her by her locker. Locker #48, cornflower blue. "What's going on?"

Her face was flush as she slammed the locker shut.

"I need to know," I said.

"It just won't work out."

"You need to tell me what's up."

"I just can't handle another thing in my life."

"What's that supposed to mean?"

She kept walking as I followed her out to her car.

"I just can't right now." She didn't look at me as she said this but stared off into the distance.

Hardcore denial on my part followed. She couldn't possibly mean it. She'd change her mind. She *had* to know we were right together. Instead, it ended up feeling like swimming in Lake Michigan, and the warm water temperatures turned into the sharp cold autumn water temperatures that prick your skin like a thousand needles.

Chapter 52

Friday rolls around and I go to the county building for my shadow to meet Mr. Green.

He's this pudgy guy wearing a gray suit and red tie. Again, props to Kenzinger for hooking me up, although, to be honest, I don't know what to expect and "job shadowing" someone working for the government doesn't exactly sound glamorous, unless he's going to reveal some secrets.

His position is kind of confusing to be perfectly honest. He gives me a run-down of it. He talks about the jail. He attends numerous meetings and works with rehabilitating prisoners and preventing the youth of America from falling to the same fate.

The shadow begins with a tour of the jail. I scramble writing down notes as he does this.

"Basically, we have the whole jail color-coded from low-risk inmates to inmates considered more high-risk," he says.

"What did the high-risk inmates do?"

He gives me a weird look. "A variety of crimes, but generally they're more unpredictable. Or we base it on the behavior from their time here."

"Do you have many high-risk inmates here?"

"Some."

I look at the chart.

I think about Women and Minorities. How a white man and a Black man can do the same crime but receive drastically different sentences. I don't mention this, even though I recall the article I read on how a study showed the differences in common drug possession sentences and the number of years solely—while not exclusively a deciding factor—can be correlated to race.

We go to an elevator.

A big muscular guy with many tattoos who looks like he could bench press me and then split my body over his knee steps out with a guard. The prisoner is not in cuffs or any restraints. Both look surprised to see us.

The guard takes a step in front of me. I graciously take a step back.

Next, we go to this meeting. He introduces me to the people and the names don't stick nor do their roles. They're going to talk about a preventative drug program is what I'm informed.

"D.A.R.E. has proven unsuccessful on many fronts," a lady, I assume the leader of the meeting, says.

Drug. Abuse. Resistance. Education. A program they made all of us take in fifth grade.

"The data shows the drug use in the surrounding schools, all of which have had the program, appear ineffective. Some of the data indicates drug use has increased."

A page is handed out analyzing their findings. My school ranks fifth on the list and I wonder if it's a mistake. Next, I wonder how they accurately gathered this data and think of an anonymous school survey they asked us to take. I told them I did cocaine since the age of five. Have done heroine and meth in the last year. And my height was seven foot ten and I weighed 350 pounds.

"There has to be a reason behind why this program is failing," a concerned elderly man in a black suit says.

They all appear baffled. Completely and utterly befuddled.

A common saying around other school districts is, *If you want to talk about drugs go to Muskegon, if you actually want to do drugs go to Lakewood High.*

"We're definitely introducing the program early enough," somebody adds.

"Maybe we need to provide a more extensive program." Oh, believe me, it was extensive enough and went on for months.

"The program is extensive enough and the children are warned about the dangers," someone else chimes in.

"The data shows it's not working."

It's interesting Orchard View and Reese Puffer—neighboring schools—rank ahead of Lakewood in drug use. Nobody asks for my input, so I remain silent. Even though I could solve this problem for them or shed new light on it. I could tell them the program was introduced to me in elementary school. They instructed us to turn down hits from blunts before we even knew what a blunt was. None of us had the slightest goddamn idea what they were talking about. We were introduced to this black and white concept "drugs=bad; no drugs=good." They patted us on the back and said we were good little boys and girls. The information became irrelevant because it didn't apply to our nine or ten-year-old lives.

After the meeting dwindles and everybody takes off, Mr. Green turns to me. "It's all about students like you." For a second, I look up, wondering if I give off those stoner vibes, but he cracks a smile.

"Ha. Ha," I say and my laugh sounds fake even to me.

Chapter 53

As I'm sometimes invited to do, I decide to attend a party on the weekend. This time it's a cross-cultural party. When I say this I don't mean what Mr. Gardner refers to in Women & Minorities: I mean there will be people from other schools there. Most notably, Reese Puffer kids. They're similar to Lakewood kids and probably the school that resembles us most similarly. They have a great band program, suck at football—when both sides play each other it is referred to as The Toilet Bowl; both sides will go without winning a game the entire season but fight for the one victory against each other and normally it will be a close game—and have a great hockey program.

They're similar to us but with key differences: most of them aren't as good looking, and they're far less intelligent. I don't say the last part spiteful. It's backed up by comparing our SAT scores and overall testing.

It's a drive to North Muskegon, in the middle of nowhere. The party was Carmen's idea and she wanted me to tag along. She offered to drive. On the drive up, I bring up Braline. She stole my weed a few months back. At the time I was pissed, but this was before I found out what happened to her.

All of us were standing in a circle, smoking in her garage. I must admit my tolerance was extremely low at this time. All of a sudden, she pointed to her neighbor's balcony and yelled, "That lady saw us. She's going to call the cops."

This led to a scramble inside. The paranoia of smoking. Somewhere in all the confusion my pot that was sitting on the counter in the garage vanished. I didn't even realize it until the next day—that's how out of it I was.

Braline went to a party at the beginning of the year. Everything I heard was second-hand through others. She got *drunk*. I'm talking beyond drunk. She was with two older guys, seniors. They both took turns raping her. She was too drunk to even scream or move. She woke up covered in their semen. When I found this out, I didn't even care about my weed.

"Why wouldn't she even want to press charges?" I ask Carmen.

"Sometimes it's not that simple. Then for real everybody would know. Then she'd have to prove it. It would be very public, and she'd end up always being the girl that got raped at that party by two guys."

"I love the gentlemen at our school. They're gentlemen and scholars."

"Not everybody is like that," Carmen says. "You're not like that."

Silence fills the air for a bit.

"I never know what to expect with their parties, but it will be fun. We'll get to meet more people."

"Oh joy."

"Don't be so glib."

"Look at you. Must be brushing up on the dictionary."

"I mean I can't always be as good as the famous Mr. McCarthy with his striking vocabulary and wit."

"Few are."

She gives me a playful jab.

"You're lucky I believe in chivalry and could never hit you back."

"You wouldn't hit me ever." The way she says this makes me feel a warmth inside.

This is where most of my male peers would reference striking a girl across the face with their appendage, but I'm simply not as crude as my male counterparts.

"Hopefully this party doesn't get busted."

"It better not. I'm too cute for prison."

She makes a pouty face and I can't deny the irritable cuteness she's alluding to.

The party is in a house similar to one you'd find in my neighborhood in Lakewood—a house with a few bedrooms and bathrooms, a double garage, but nothing noteworthy.

The majority of people are in the garage.

When met by the host, we are introduced, and the usual banter anytime somebody from rivalry schools commences.

"Nice you could make it," The Host, Aaron, says, sarcastically.

"I assume you will live up to your name, Puffer, and be smoking the ganja," I say.

"We do have weed," he informs me.

Later on, I make my way to the kitchen. I've had a few vodka drinks and I'm feeling pretty good. Parties are weird. All these people randomly talking. Dozens of conversations going on at once. Sometimes you barely remember what's said.

Sometimes it's overwhelming and I need to sit in a corner.

"How's it going?" Aaron asks, standing by all of the bottles lined up.

"Could be drunker," I admit.

"Going to get lucky tonight?"

"Not planning on it."

He gives me this weird look I can't decipher.

Carmen walks into the kitchen. "I need another drink. What's good?" she asks me.

"Vodka."

"But with what?"

Aaron swoops in. "I'd recommend vodka with orange soda."

"It's called pop," I say.

He gives me a funny look. "What are the sleeping arrangements going to be tonight? You sleeping with your girl?"

"She's not my girl."

I want to punch him in the face, and this is why I hate Reece Puffer kids.

"I mean I can take her off your hands. It's not like I haven't spent the night with her before."

"What do you mean?"

"I mean we slept together."

"She hasn't slept with anybody."

"I didn't say we had sex. Maybe this time we will." He looks me dead in the eyes and smirks. "I mean there's a first time for everything."

"You don't know what you're talking about."

"Stop." Carmen pushes between us.

"What's he mean?"

"Just drop it. Both of you." She glares.

"What the hell is going on?"

"Just saying I shared a bed with her," Aaron says. "No need to get worked up."

"Is he?" I ask. "The guy in his boxers?"

"Yes," she mutters. "Stop. Both of you."

I look him in the eyes when I say, "The only way you'll ever get a girl in bed is if you force her to or say she has to. Someday we'll see you on *To Catch a Predator* when you're older."

"At least I can get a girl in bed."

"Everybody in your school thinks you're like us, but you're not. You are poorer, uglier, and clearly stupider. SAT scores back this up."

I realize at this point there's a crowd around us and we are the center of the show. I notice a few mean looks after I say this.

"At least in my school we know the difference between guys and girls," Aaron says.

"What's that supposed to mean?"

"It means we don't let fags prance around our school like you do. If we have a penis, we know it. We don't switch teams. And we don't let girls pretend like they do."

"All of your teams are losing," Carmen chimes in.

I go in for the final blow. "Your dad left your mom because she couldn't stand to see you turn into the same douchebag your father is."

Aaron lunges at me but the guys around him hold him back.

Naturally, we leave right after. Neither of us wanted to stay for obvious reasons. We don't talk as we make our exit to the car. We pull out and Carmen lets out a sigh.

"That guy was a real dick, wasn't he?" I say after a few minutes of driving. Carmen leaves her hands on the wheel and keeps her eyes ahead on the road.

The silence lasts for a good thirty seconds.

"Right?" I ask.

Carmen's mouth pushes together like she's grinding her teeth.

"I'd be pissed too," I add.

I notice the shift in acceleration of the vehicle.

"Talk to me. Tell me what's on your mind."

She doesn't say anything.

"Don't do this to me. I can't stand the silence."

She still doesn't say anything.

"Friggen talk to me."

She pulls over into the rest stop without saying a word. She gets out of the car and slams the door. I follow her. It's pitch black out.

"You're an asshole," Carmen says.

"I'm an asshole? *I'm* an asshole?"

"You don't need to tell everybody I slept with a guy in his boxers."

"It wasn't even your choice though."

"I know, but it *sounds* bad."

"He started the fight."

"I don't care who started it."

And I still wish I was the guy in boxers sleeping with Carmen.

"Why'd you even say yes?"

"I was drunk and stupid. They told me I had to. Again, *nothing* happened."

"I want to go back and set their house on fire."

"Like that will change the past."

"Why do you like assholes so much? Maybe if you had better judgment this wouldn't have happened."

"You had no right to make a scene. I told you that, just between you and me. I haven't even told my friends about that. Alexis knows because she was at the party, but that's it. How can I tell you anything anymore?"

"That's not fair."

"You doing that to me wasn't fair. I thought *you* weren't like that."

And this stings.

We get back into the car.

Silence permeates.

"I didn't mean to ..." I begin

Carmen doesn't say anything.

"You *can* tell me anything," I say. "We tell each other everything."

Carmen lets out an aggravated sigh as she glares at the road ahead.

We don't talk the rest of the drive home.

Chapter 54

"She got out," Pops says frantically when I get home.

"What do you mean?"

"I opened the door for a second and she ran out. Goddamn it!" he yells.

"She always comes back," I point out, not entirely sure if she wants to.

She's a free spirit.

"If she doesn't want me she can just stay out there, goddamn it," he says.

"Maybe she wants to be free." Completely uninhibited by societal norms, boring rules, and caged in a prison where everybody acts like they're doing it for your own benefit when it's only another method of physical restraint and thought control.

My dad looks at me like I suggested sure death.

"Do you hear it?" He jumps up like a deranged person. *Oh, shit. This time he really lost it.*

"What?"

"The meows."

"I don't hear anything."

I'm going to have to put him in a home sooner than I thought. I'll tell him they'll take very good care of him. I debate leafing through the phone book to find numbers for mental institutions. I wonder if they would put him in a white straight jacket and take him away.

"Can you at least help me look?"

He sprints to the door.

"Are you sure you're not just imagining them?"

"I hear them, the meows."

My dad bolts out the door, running around the back yard like a goddamn lunatic. I hope the neighbors aren't witnessing his psychosis.

Then I hear them. The meows. Faint.

"Come here," Pops commands.

I attempt to call her in, but softer, cooing her.

She appears, climbing over the fence. Making her way to us. I run out and scoop her up.

"She came back. My little girl. We need to get her warmed up."

A part of me wonders if she's better off living the life she wants. Hunting birds and mice like she was before. Roaming free where her heart desires. Climbing fences and trees. Making her own decisions.

Chapter 55

The snow started to clear up and has turned into a dirty slush with pools of water on the street and mounds of snow left from the places the snowplows piled up the snow during the long winter. Of course, it being Michigan and all, we never really know if winter is done. It's not uncommon for it to snow in April.

Today, we're visiting gramps again. I agreed not to be as hard on the old geezer this time.

"Sometimes you have to learn when to ignore people," Pops says on the drive there. "He doesn't always know what he's saying."

We arrive and his house smells like grandpa. Musty. Like old skin and decaying flesh.

"I'm making us some steak," Gramps says.

I set the table and retreat to the other room. The T.V. is on as it always is. Some stupid reality show where they just complain about living in an expensive apartment with a bunch of others, are given all the food they need to survive, but can't manage to get along.

"I was driving to the store today," Gramps says. "And this guy pulls out in front of me and cuts me off. I drove around him and gave him the bird."

I start laughing. Out of all the words possible to come out of his mouth, this was the least I expected and from him of all people.

The steak is overcooked. It's like chewing on leather.

Pops gets up to go to the bathroom.

Pops always tells me not to talk about mom with Gramps too much because it will "upset" him. In my later years, I've obliged and dropped the subject.

Tonight, I feel like pushing the envelope a bit.

"How old was I when I went to the ocean with my mom and dad?" I ask.

Gramps looks at me like I said elephants can fly. Or like I'm high.

"Didn't we go on a trip when I was younger?" I press.

"I don't know what you're talking about." He looks puzzled.

Pops walks back into the room. And I am done inquiring on the subject.

Later, we play three-handed Euchre. If there's one game that's native to Michigan, it's Euchre.

"Your grandma used to love playing Euchre," he says. I think about how if my grandma didn't ditch us for Florida, we'd have enough people to play four handed. I wonder sometimes if he misses her or not, but he doesn't talk about it. Something to do with being a man of few words and a part of the Silent Generation which doesn't care to talk about much of anything and the most noticeable thing they did was hump like rabbits and create a bunch of kids.

"Everybody in the family used to love it. I'd play every Sunday with my brother and sister." He looks out the window like he is thinking about something. "Those were the days."

On account of my dad also being the only child and me not having a mother, we never have any family get togethers.

"You play Euchre well," Gramps tells me. "Do you kids play in school?"

"Sometimes."

We go on streaks where we decide to play at lunch randomly, but it's not an everyday kind of occurrence.

For the rest of the evening, he doesn't go on any racist rants, comment about Mexicans or Black people, and it's not too bad of an evening to be honest with you.

Chapter 56

Carmen and I don't talk for the remainder of the weekend. I send her AIM messages pleading with her to talk to me, but I don't get a single response. I call her house only to be told from her dad she's not home—although I don't know if I believe him.

It makes me think of when we didn't talk anymore. Complete silence for an entire month.

I remember around Christmas time, when the end of the semester approached. Carmen and I both sang in the choir—an easy elective neither of us expressed much interest in—and we had to sing in the annual Singing Christmas Tree. It's in some huge catholic church St. Something or Another, and it's this big deal.

Attendance is mandatory.

It's literally how it sounds. This big huge Christmas tree with places for the kids to stand in the tree, and it's high in the air because the building is tall. Looking up by the building itself you get vertigo.

The snow came down fluffy. Not the heavy hard kind good for packing snowballs or building snowman, but the movie kind that makes it look like you're living in a snow globe.

Normally, at least three kids pass out during the performances over the course of the four days we do them. Well, I wasn't feeling well to begin with. Despite all this, I wasn't one of the kids that passed out. That'd be Taylor Larcen, Cory Perry, and Jeana Norris. Carmen came over after our last performance.

My dad left us alone in the living room. She massaged my back, her hands under my shirt, despite me being all sticky and sweaty and sick. This was after the whole her establishing not wanting a boyfriend part. She didn't even say anything. We let the T.V. play and she kept rubbing my back, making me feel better.

The snow kept coming down outside the window.

"I'm sorry," Carmen said, barely audible. In a way, I had started getting sick before this. Throwing up some mornings and really upset. I knew it was because of Carmen. I had envisioned a whole big grand future in my head and thought she was going to be my girlfriend.

"For what?"

"Everything."

"It's not your fault I'm sick."

I tried glancing at her but she looked away, still massaging me. Her hands felt good, firm and not soft.

"I know ..." She trailed off.

"What do you know?"

"Maybe not much of anything."

Her voice sounded sad. Sometimes out of nowhere this melancholy appeared in her, making me wonder if it was always hidden below the surface. But here it surfaced like that.

Her hands pushed into my back harder. She squeezed my shoulders.

"I've never massaged a boy before," she laughed.

"You're doing a good job."

I felt a little better but still super sick. I thought of words I could say. Sometimes I'll still go back and think of words I should have said. But I'm not sure any of it would have changed anything or even mattered. She had made up her mind. The reasoning was never quite clear. One second she acted like she was all in. The next she wasn't.

I don't even like to talk about it with anyone. I didn't have anyone to talk about it with. My grades dropped slightly but I managed to bring them back up. We never talked about the past or our date.

But I'll still remember that night. Her hands on my back. The snow falling slowly outside. Feeling sick but she was there, and it made everything better.

Chapter 57

I arrive early to Physics. Carmen's attendance is always questionable. Sometimes she's early. Sometimes right on time. Other times late.

When I get to class, I see exactly what I wanted: Carmen sitting down at her table. Barely anybody else in the class. Nobody sitting at her table.

I sit down next to her.

She looks at me then looks away.

"So ..." I lead.

"I got all of your messages and read them."

"I'm sorry. I didn't mean to betray your trust."

She lets out a sigh.

"I get if you're still mad at me, and I want to make it up to you and—"

She shushes me with her finger. "Just shh," she says. "I'll forgive you, but we have to keep working on this."

As much as a part of me still wants it—will always want it—I know she isn't talking about our "relationship" and some romantic future with walks on the beach or where she wears my sweatshirts in the fall.

"Work on what?" I ask. I need clarity.

"Avery."

"We can do that."

Everything feels better all at once.

"How did you know his mother left his dad?" Carmen asks.

"There was only one picture up of them when he was younger and all the rest were only pictures of him and his dad."

"You realize his dad could have left his mom, right?"

"I took an educated guess."

Chapter 58

How do votes get miscounted?

To explore this matter, I didn't have to dive in as deeply as I thought. Perhaps there was some kind of delicate process where the votes went through numerous hands, anonymity was preserved, and a flawless system was in place?

Votes are student counted. The most common in first hour and sixth hour to help with office work. Traditionally, first hour runs out all the notes for students with doctor notes; sixth hour helps with other matters. It's not even uncommon for the school to make them pick up trash in the school parking lot in the warmer months.

Generally, sixth hour arranges events. They plan the school dances. Decorate them, and as it happens: conduct the completion of student-based surveys—such as the one for Snow Coming King and Queen. The hours in between generally have one or two "helpers" but not many people like first or sixth hour.

Carmen explains all of this to me as we sit at a desolate lunch table (students are never here *this* early). We're hanging out before class—both of us arrived ungodly early, a full hour before classes to plan and to catch Mr. Cannon in his best mood (the beginning of the day).

"How do you know all of this?" I ask.

"I have my ways," she says.

"You know we could be wrong about everything." A truth I must point out; maybe Avery didn't win.

"I don't buy it. Everybody I talked to said they voted for Avery."

"You're using confirmation bias where you only apply your views to what you see in front of you."

Carmen rolls her eyes.

"Besides we can't fall victim to selection bias when surveying students."

"I know, that's why you got me. I can talk to anybody."

The last part still remains a characteristic of slight envy.

"You're not impressing me with your big words, Mr. McCarthy."

I approach Mr. Cannon before his first hour starts. "I believe there may have been possible fraudulent proceedings in the Lakewood High 2007 Snow Coming Election," I start.

After taking a gulp of his coffee, he asks, "How can we be so sure? Are you basing this off of who your friends would have picked?"

"I'll conduct a survey of over 50 students today alone."

"Part of democracy also is the confidentiality of the voters," he adds, looking at me.

"Let's make sure though. Say I conduct a survey and we find more than 50%, maybe even more than 75% of the students surveyed said they voted for Avery would that prove my point?" When speaking with adults sometimes cliches must be added. "Or would it raise eyebrows so to speak?"

"I'd be leery of your methods, but I would be interested in the results," I swear for a second he smiles then it goes away.

The follow up question: *Who is tallying up these votes?* The question proceeding this question: *Who the hates Avery so much to make him lose?*

The obvious candidates are the others who were elected for Snow Coming King and Queen.

"I'll make sure the surveys are given to a wide variety of the student body. No confirmation bias here."

"You have until the end of the day," Mr. Cannon says.

We make a survey. We're optimistic and print out 100 surveys asking the students to vote anonymously. The librarian glares at us despite there being no cap limit on the number of pages a student is allowed to print.

"Are people going to actually be willing to answer the survey?" I ask.

"You underestimate people," Carmen says. She takes 65 surveys; I take 35.

"Why do you get more?" I ask.

"Because I know more people."

At the day's conclusion, I conduct a total of 15. Most people ignored me or didn't want to participate.

"I found plenty of people willing to take the survey from all social circles and grade levels," Carmen announces.

We didn't see each other at all today—except before school, in the library, and Physics—due to us scrambling around, attempting to survey students. I get she tries seeing the good in everybody and all that, but sometimes it's hard for me to see it.

The vote totals 74. The unsurprising results:

Avery Bowen: 54

Bret Ellen: 20.

Chapter 59

In Women and Minorities, we drive to Lincoln Park, my old elementary school to share our stories. I ride with Alex and Lily in the car. Lily and I ride in the back.

"What's this for?" she asks.

"It's for work," Alex says. "My price tag gun."

She starts sticking price tags on the seat. She sticks one on me. "How much are you worth?"

"Stop that," Alex says.

She sticks another sticker on him.

We arrive at the school and it's so *different* than I remember it from the super small tubs to the micro-sized lockers, to the micro-sized students.

"Was it always this small?" Lily asks, reading my mind.

"I don't remember it being like this," I say.

We go to the classroom, and I see Mr. Arnold my fourth-grade teacher. The same fourth-grade classroom I was in when I was nine. I look at the tiny tubs and remember how my favorite number is seven because Rachel's tub number was seven. It all feels and looks so different from the miniature tables to the tiny chairs.

The kids themselves look so small, and I don't remember feeling that small when I was their age.

"Class, we're going to have these kind students read you some stories," Mr. Arnold says.

Story time used to be one of my favorite times of the day. We'd sit on the floor Indian style in a line and draw on each other's backs with our fingers and take turns switching so everybody would get a turn. Doing things like that didn't seem weird at the time. I remember trading Jolly Ranchers for Pokémon cards. Playing soccer at recess and the game turning into rugby when somebody would pick up the ball. Touch football—sometimes tackle if the chaperons weren't paying attention—and kickball. We'd eat War Heads that were intensely sour. I remember diving into the snow after eating them and snowball fights.

It was a completely different life.

We take turns reading our stories and Alex reads ours about the blue bunny who couldn't fit in and was made fun of because he was blue and had super long blue ears. Lily looks at me and smiles. It all feels kind of strange to be perfectly honest with you. Weird how time changes things and how we look at things change and once we were these kids in the classroom. We used to imagine driving around in cars one day with girlfriends, having everything figured out. Dream of being football players, actors, or astronauts.

But maybe it isn't as easy as we used to think. The world's more confusing than we imagined.

Chapter 60

I visit Tommy after school. I notice how I visit him less and less as the years pass. We used to play every single day when I was a kid.

"Soon you won't know anybody who's in high school," Tommy says. "I don't know anybody who is there now. That's how it goes."

And it's a weird thought having little to zero connections in a building I once roamed every day, wasted countless hours of my life, became involuntarily imprisoned in, and subjected to scrupulous mind control and "educational" requirements while being stripped of most of my individuality.

"I look forward to it."

"You say that now but it's not like it's as easy out there to make friends. It's not like how it was then or how it was with the kids in the neighborhood."

By default, we all played together, spent our summers together without questioning it whatsoever, like it was meant to be.

"It was weird going back there today," I say. I remember when Tommy stood up for me. My walk was only a short one from elementary school, but a few bullies would sit by the sidewalk, waiting to push me into the snow. They'd take turns and each time I'd get up another one would push me down. They'd taunt me.

One time there was yellow snow.

They pushed me into it. They laughed.

"You ate dog pee."

Tommy was there. A quick snowball hit their leader in the face. He started crying.

"Leave him alone," Tommy said.

One of the other kids charged him. Tommy took him to the ground and pushed him headfirst into the ground, making him eat snow. He rubbed the snow onto the face with his gloves. A whitewash.

"How do you like it now?" he asked.

All of the kids ran away and never picked on me again.

"Life's not like high school," Tommy says. "It's messy. It's not as clean."

"Why?"

"It doesn't get any easier."

It occurs to me: somebody needs to stick up for Avery the same way Tommy stood up for me. The same way Carmen stood up for Ed.

Chapter 61

Sometimes there comes a point in a young man's life where he needs answers. Unfortunately, these times don't always come when ideally fit. I knock on Carmen's door.

"Why didn't it work out?" Not the strongest lead, and I should have built up to it. But I *have* to know. Am I just someone she doesn't see as a good match? Does she have her eyes on someone else?

"What do you mean?" She looks at her feet then back at me.

"You know exactly what I mean. You acted like you liked me oh so much then all of a sudden decided I wasn't worth the time of day to you. Yet you'll still talk to me all the time, flirt with me, even hint at sexual stuff."

"It's just complicated."

"That's a cop out if I ever heard one. Everything is just oh-so-complicated."

"Okay, come in."

I follow her to her bedroom where we sit on the bed. A part of me wonders if I'm making a mistake. If this is an issue that shouldn't be forced. But I need answers goddamn it.

"You're unusually quiet," I observe. "Normally, you have an opinion on every goddamn thing ever."

She looks down, like she's noticing patterns in her bed sheets she hadn't noticed before.

"It is complicated," she says again.

"Doesn't seem like we're making any real progress here. I want to know. Am I not good enough?"

"You are good enough. This isn't about anybody's ego. I just ... I just ..."

"Spill it."

"I can't."

"Okay, sounds like impeccable logic based on lots of intrinsic thought."

"You realize I've never had an actual boyfriend before, like a real boyfriend, right? It's not like I have all these answers."

I sigh.

I want her to say she likes somebody else. Or she realizes she's a lesbian. Or something I can wrap my head around or at least attempt to. Or that she still has a stupid little crush on me.

"There's more to it than that," she says at last. "It's not like I had a lot of good relationships to model my life around with my parents. My cousin, my best friend's boyfriend treats her like crap, lies to her, and cheats on her."

"Don't see what that has to do with us. It's not like I have solid parental figures who stayed together. It's another cop out. Another goddamn excuse."

A tear trickles down her cheek.

"Listen, I'm sorry. I ... it's like you remind me of how I failed with you always," I say, feeling kind of bad.

"I'm not just some conquest to check off your bucket list. Like, oh, the first girl you got to kiss or do stuff with."

"I wanted you to be more than any of that."

Carmen asks me to meet her at Lake Harbor. She doesn't say anything when she gets out of the car. I follow her. We walk until we're sitting by the channel that flows from Mona Lake into Lake Michigan. The same place I used to feed ducks with Gramps.

She called me and told me to meet her here. Her voice sounded expressionless.

"What did you want to tell me?"

"There's something I need to tell you," Carmen repeats. Her expression looks blank for a second as she peers into the channel. The water ripples and even manages to look cold.

She looks back at me, sad, her lower lip trembles, but not in the pouty way when she's asking something from me.

"Yes?" I lean in closer.

She breathes in heavy. "I know I told you that I've never given a blow job, but ... I have."

"What?"

I run through lists of guys she's talked to, guys who went by her locker. Luke Hanson comes to mind, and I've always suspected they had a thing for each other.

"Before you get mad know it wasn't by choice."

"Huh?"

"When I was younger, probably about 11, a friend of my dad's made me do it. It was at the old house when he had people over. His friend told me I had to do it. No matter how much I cried he grabbed my head and kept saying, *This is what all the good girls do.*"

A silence lingers.

"I know you're probably mad ..."

"I am."

I feel the redness creep into my face and the muscles in my neck restrict. The last time I felt like this was when I pushed Connor into the locker.

"I wanted you to be my first," she says. Tears trickle down her cheeks.

"It doesn't count," I let out a breath. "I just hate whoever the guy is."

"You're not mad at me?"

"Jesus. Of course not. I want to hurt whoever he is."

"I don't want anybody to know."

"It's rape."

"I don't want to just become the girl that got mouth raped to everyone."

"Nobody will think that."

"But they will. And that's all I'll ever be to them. When they see me, they'll think, *That's the girl that gave blow jobs when she was 11.*"

She looks at me again and it hurts seeing her in pain.

It looks like the water picked up in the channel.

"Why didn't you tell your dad?"

"I didn't think he would believe me." She looks at the ground. "And then if he actually did, he would've killed the guy. Then he would have been in jail for the rest of his life, and I wouldn't have had a father."

I can't think of a reply for this because in a way I know it's true, but I want justice. I want to live in a fair world.

"Promise me you won't tell anybody." She's solemn.

"Who would I tell?"

"Promise me. I haven't told anybody."

And we share in each other's darkness. I would have never guessed in a million years that Carmen, this happy smiling girl, a social butterfly, has this dark secret she didn't choose.

"I won't tell anybody. But you know that."

Chapter 62

When I see Benson sitting at a table in the lunchroom it all comes together. His sixth hour slack class. The same one that performs duties to help out with student affairs. Affairs such as the Snow Coming Dance. Meaning he and the others in his class were responsible for counting votes.

Without thinking I storm to his table. He's sitting alone.

"I know what you did," I say.

He looks at me. "What are you talking about?"

"Don't play stupid. I'm not saying you acted alone."

He doesn't say anything.

"It's no secret how much you hate Avery. He's different. I know. You couldn't let him win. You miscounted the votes. You hate anybody who's gay, transgender, or anything different. It's not like you've hidden your stance on that."

"What are you saying?"

"Is it really such a coincidence that the class you're in, your *slack class*, where you got to count votes for the election, that somehow Avery didn't end up winning?"

"What are you saying?" He stands up, angry.

"You know damn well what I'm saying."

"I don't."

"You rigged the election. You purposely didn't count votes for Avery because you couldn't stand to see a transgender person win."

"I did no such thing." I can't read his expression, but he looks at the ground for a second.

"I find that extremely hard to believe."

There's silence, and instead of talking he's staring into space, like he's contemplating something.

"I'm offering you a chance to defend yourself or explain what happened when you were counting votes."

"It wasn't me." He shifts uncomfortably. "I don't know how but Bret Ellen won, I swear."

"Even Bret doesn't think he had enough people to win."

"He didn't," Benson mutters under his breath.

"Was that a confession of guilt?" I ask. "There's no way you know *nothing* about what went on."

He doesn't say anything and stares off.

"See. I figured it out."

"It wasn't me."

"Then if not you, then who?"

He looks at me, serious. "Some of what you're saying is true. But I'm not the one who changed anything."

"Like what?"

"Avery did win the election by popular vote."

"Why did you change it?"

"I. DID. NOT. CHANGE. ANYTHING." The anger flairs under his eyes.

"Then who did? It's not like this is a coincidence."

"It didn't come from any students. We delivered the count straight to Principal Harris."

Chapter 63

As Mr. Cannon informed all of us, some interviews are harder than others. People are defensive, even more so when they have something to hide. They become guarded. They'll give you perversions of the truth and misdirect information to purposely steer you in the wrong direction. Sometimes more aggressive approaches become necessary when prying information from somebody.

"I need to speak with Principal Harris," I say to Mrs. Penski.

She looks up at me. "Do you have an appointment?"

"Not exactly, but I think he'll want to talk to me. It's urgent for an article and I have to clear something up."

I can tell the request annoys her.

"I'll check and see if he's available," she says.

She disappears for a second. I prepped a few questions but am acutely aware this is one of the most difficult interviews I'll ever conduct. I wish time was on my side—but the longer I wait the more time the administration has for their cover-up.

"He says he's busy right now and wants to set up a time next week," she informs me.

"I can't wait for this. It's urgent for an article for the paper. It's about the Snow Coming King and Queen. I can explain it to him. It's for an article. I need to confirm a few pieces of information. It will only take five minutes."

"I'll tell him." She retreats again.

Mr. Cannon said lying to interviewees—especially about your intentions of the said interview—is risky. It often leads to a lack of cooperation. I debated telling Harris the article discussed the misuse of illicit substances in sports. If I said it was about politics in sports, I know I'd have an even worse shot of getting him to speak to me.

"He'll see you," she says. "But he wants you to know he doesn't have much time."

Principal Harris looks worse close up, more like a corpse who barely came back to life. His purple tie stands out, bright. His head wrinkles, and his hair looks more white than gray.

"How may I help you today, Mr. McCarthy?"

"I wanted to talk to you about Snow Coming."

Principal Harris looks at me cautiously. "What about it?"

"You announced that Bret Ellen was the winner. There must be some kind of mistake. *Everybody* voted for Avery."

Journalism at its essence is supposed to merely be the fly on the wall, the unbiased observer. Always provide people with the opposing viewpoint an opportunity to defend themselves or offer their take on it.

His brow wrinkles and I can't decipher his expression.

"Bret Ellen won the vote. While I must admit it was close, it's just how the votes tallied up."

"Did they?"

A look of shock sweeps over his face then anger. His brow wrinkle deepens, and I can't tell if he knows I know.

He lets out a breath. "The results are as stands."

"Who counted the votes?"

"I don't get what you are getting at here …"

"It was brought to my attention that Avery received the majority of the popular vote and when the results were turned in, somehow that changed." I add, "I have a very reliable source."

Avoid yes or no questions unless confirming details, such as facts for the articles.

"I see," he says, thinking.

I don't say anything else. I stare at him. People hate awkward silences and want to fill the air with words. Mr. Cannon walked us through many journalistic strategies. By far, the most effective is silence. Ask somebody a question, when they provide a minimalistic response, don't utter a syllable. Look at them. They'll start to get uncomfortable. Nine out of ten times they'll provide more information.

"I appreciate your support for your friend, but I can't change the results."

"I think you should have some kind of recount. I can help. I took a general un-biased survey for the article I'm working on for the school paper, and I think it hints there may have been some interference in the Snow Coming vote."

"We can't do that," he says.

"Is it possible the results were tampered?"

"I'd be extremely careful about making sweeping generalizations, Mr. McCarthy." I look him in the eyes, and I know he knows. He knows I know. He looks down first. "Also, I'd be cautious about what you print in the school paper. It's to my understanding that you've already been issued several warnings."

Save the most difficult questions for last. Until the end of the interview. It's possible the subject will back out or end the interview.

"Did the administration change the results?"

"Absolutely not."

I pause. Silence. I hope he'll spill more, but he appears hard as a statue.

"Leave it as it is." His eyes are cold.

"But in all fairness—"

"We don't need any more confusion among impressionable young people."

"What do you mean *confusion?*"

"Is Avery a boy or a girl, do we even know? It's too much confusion for young impressionable minds," he says, sounding like a douchebag reading from an article published in the 1960s about sexually troubled teenagers.

"So, you're saying you changed the results?"

"I have nothing more to say on the subject."

"I think that answers the question."

I get up to leave.

When I get to the door, he says, "We are a small community. We can't cause trouble. It's not the school's job to rile people up."

I storm to Carmen's locker. She's talking to her friends. "I need to talk to you in private."

She holds up a hand to me.

"Now."

The urgency in my voice rushes out and sounds harsher than I intend. The two girls give me irritated looks.

"Alright, Mr. Grumpy, what's the deal?"

"He knows. It was all on purpose. They changed the vote."

"What? Why?"

"I can tell."

"How do you know?"

"He said, *It's too much confusion for impressionable minds.* Then talked about how Avery doesn't even know if he's a boy or a girl."

"Jesus."

"That's probably their biggest reason behind it."

"Don't say it like that."

Blood rushes to my head; I punch the locker next to me.

Chapter 64

I'm not familiar with everybody else's writing process for the *Lakewood Bi-Weekly*, but I can picture it. I'm sure Jeanna Smith prays before she writes. Carl Denton probably scratches his balls and has that stupid clueless look on his face he's known for. Blane Connely probably has a calculated outline of every point he will make in chronological order. I can see Mr. Cannon in his younger years—but still rocking the gray beard—with a glass of scotch in his hand, completely focused on writing his article which involved heavy sleuthing.

To say I have a set way of writing my article would be an overstatement. Generally, I'm sitting by my desktop (surprisingly not smoking pot or drinking alcohol), and it kind of just comes to me. Normally, I'm writing the damn thing in my head all week. With this one, I don't have a set plan. Before I started writing articles, I had to hardcore convince my dad to have the desktop in my bedroom. It's not like he uses the damn thing anyway. He thought I'd watch kiddie porn on it.

I reassured him I'd only watch regular porn on it, and he rolled his eyes.

I've stuck to my word.

I call up Benson. For some reason I have his number and don't remember getting it.

"Can I use what you said in the article I'm writing?" I ask. A loaded question for sure, but for some reason I feel this obligatory journalistic responsibility.

"Don't say that I said it," he says.

"It'll make it sound more legit."

"Keep my name out of it. I don't want to get into any trouble."

"But I could at least say I heard from a reputable source?"

"I guess."

I organize all the information I have. What Benson told me, our survey, and my conversation with Principal Harris.

Then I let it come together in my head and write:

Snow Coming Election Fraud?

As many of you know, Bret Ellen won the Snow Coming King vote. However, there may be more to this story than meets the eye. Avery Bowen ran for Snow Coming King as well. This may come as a shock to some of you (or not) but there is evidence the election results may have been tampered with.

A reliable source (who chooses to be unnamed) confirmed Bowen won the popular vote, and these votes were delivered straight to Principal Harris. These votes were tallied up by this individual and others.

An unbiased survey conducted of 74 students of numerous backgrounds, grades, and sexes backed this up as well:

Avery Bowen: 54

Bret Ellen: 20

While this doesn't mean Bowen won the Snow Coming vote, it does provide an accurate sample of the student vote.

Principal Harris declined to comment on much of this possible election fraud scandal but did say the results are as stands. He did question however if Bowen knows whether he is a "boy" or a "girl."

Principal Harris added, "It's too much confusion for young impressionable minds."

While not directly admitting to tampering in the election, this does raise questions.

Principal Harris said, "We are a small community. We can't cause trouble. It's not the school's job to rile people up."

As this is a breaking news story, more information may come to light. Know you are in a safe community that cares very much about their image. A community that doesn't care about the truth. The question is how much is being sheltered worth to you?

As I write the last bit of the article, I know it will not only hit hard but will cause problems. I debate telling Carmen I can't carry through with it. That it will all be too much. But there's this feeling in the back, inside me, that knows if I don't reveal this truth nothing will be right again. Not just for me but for everybody in the entire school. And for all of the people around us.

Chapter 65

While Mr. Cannon is on lunch, I meet with him. He always eats alone in his room, normally either grading student papers or with a newspaper in hand. He never goes to the teacher's lounge.

He looks up at me.

"Mr. McCarthy, what can I do for you?"

"We collected a wide sample of the student vote. I attempted to interview Principal Harris, but he declined to comment on the Snow Coming Election."

"Did you plan the interview?"

"I kind of just told him I needed to meet with him."

"Sneaky, but I told you that can backfire."

"I wrote my next article. It's titled, *Snow Coming Election Fraud?* With a question mark. I included samples of the vote, and quotes from Principal Harris—"

"We can't publish it," he cuts me off firmly.

"What?"

He looks at me and I can't quite decipher the look in his eyes, maybe worn down from all the stories he covered, maybe a sad realization.

"You told us to always pursue truth at all costs and that's what journalism is about."

"I also told you that the school is not the United States. Our country guarantees us the right to freedom of the press. A school, unfortunately, does not."

"That's it? I'm just done? All the work I put in is snuffed out only because we met a little bit of resistance? The student body has the *right* to know what happened during that election."

"You don't have to write an additional article this week. It'll still count as credit."

"I don't care about that. I want my article read by the student body. I want everybody to know about this cover up."

Mr. Cannon looks at me with tired eyes, like he's trying to calculate his next words.

"While you may be right; the students have a right to know, Principal Harris specifically told me not to allow any articles related to Avery Bowen and the Snow Coming Election to be published."

"That's bullshit," I let it slip out.

"It is." Mr. Cannon nods. "It's out of my control. You'll find you can't always pursue the articles you want to. Whether it's your boss telling you not to, company politics, or something else."

"I already wrote the article. I not only put in all that work for nothing, but nobody will read it?"

"That's life," Mr. Cannon says, unsympathetically.

"That's bullshit," Carmen says when I tell her what Mr. Cannon said.

"I'm fully aware."

Everything I'm supposed to stand for as a journalist denied.

"We're going to publish your article."

"Even if I tried to publish it, I don't know how," I admit. "And you heard what Mr. Cannon said; it's not allowed."

"We're not supposed to do a lot of things. We still do them."

"*This* is different."

"And you've become such the rule follower now?"

"I respect what he said. I don't want to get him in trouble." The words sound strange coming out of my mouth.

"People *need* to read your story," Carmen says. "You've put too much time into it."

"I'll still get credit." The words sound hollow even to me.

She looks at me, pouting on purpose, knowing the gravity she has on me.

"This would be a big deal," I say. "I'd get in serious trouble."

"It *is* a big deal." She looks me squarely in the eyes, still pouting. "A very big deal."

I look down.

The administration covers up what they want to. They do as they please. It's not about truth, knowing what's going on inside the school. They care about appearances and what everything *looks* like, and they want to project the facade of thousands of smiling happy kids growing up to be real contributions to society all because of their sterling education at the pristine Lakewood High School.

"You've already came so far," she says. Carmen hugs me. I don't know why and if feels like weird timing for a hug.

"What's the hug for?"

"Shhh," she says squeezing me harder and burying her head into my chest. She feels warm and her hair smells nothing short of amazing. I put my head on her head.

"Agan, I don't know how to even get it published."

"What if I told you I know a way?"

She grabs the article from my hand.

Chapter 66

Carmen's friend can help us, or she thinks he can, but we have to play it off the right way. She knows this kid, Brandon. He helps print the paper in his first hour document design class, where he basically takes all of the documents from Word and then puts them into this program—one, which I frankly don't understand—and uses that to print newspaper articles.

"How do you know Brandon again?" I ask. I'm persistent.

"It's not like *that*. I've known him since freshman year."

I always wonder how much she's telling me and notice she hasn't talked about any past crushes but will blatantly talk bad about Rachel who she knows was my first crush. I do think she tells me quite a bit, but sometimes I question if she tells me *everything* like she says she does.

Because Carmen is sneaky and has wit, she's going to convince him that my article needs to go in.

She approaches him as I stand by her.

"We, ahh, forgot to publish an article in the paper this week. I was wondering if you could slip it in?" she asks.

Brandon looks at Carmen weird.

"Normally Mr. Cannon gives them to me if that's the case," Brandon says.

"He's at a meeting right now and couldn't give it to you. He trusts you'd understand how McCarthy here is a respectable journalist."

The art of bullshit.

"Why didn't McCarthy just come to me?" Brandon provides valid reasoning. His suspicions are high.

"I'm his best friend so I wanted to go with him," Carmen says. It's the first time she referred to us as best friends.

"Will you help us out?" I ask.

Carmen gives him her trademark manipulation tactic: her pouty face.

"Yeah, it's no problem."

"Great." Carmen hugs him.

When we walk away, Carmen says, "It was an act. Don't worry and start to get all jealous."

"I'm offended, you think I'd get jealous."

"Please, you get jealous about everything."

"And you don't?" I smile.

She looks at me. "Shut up." She playfully bumps me with her hips and I must admit they feel nice and it makes me wish she was bumping me with less clothing but I stop my mind from going too far in that direction.

Later when Carmen and I stand by her locker Brandon walks up to us.

"I can't do it," Brandon says.

"Why?" Carmen asks.

"I just can't. I'd get into too much trouble."

"But why?"

"I can't. It's not allowed."

"I didn't know you were such a pansy," Carmen yells at him as he walks away.

"Looks like your manipulation can only go so far," I observe.

Chapter 67

Mr. Cannon is late to class. I take this as a sign from the newspaper deities.

I stand up and announce to the whole class, "Mr. Cannon forbid me to publish my article on the Snow Coming vote. It turns out Avery should have won and the administration didn't let him because he's transgender. My article needs to be published."

They stare at me blankly for a few seconds.

"Students deserve to know about this," I add. "Think about it along the lines of freedom. Maybe you don't like what somebody is doing, but they still have the right to do it if they're not hurting you. Sure, maybe it makes some of you uncomfortable, but I think if you read my article, you can see Avery as a person."

"How do you know this?" Blane asks.

"I have proof in my article. I conducted a survey, interviewed Principal Harris, and have an inside source."

I distribute the article I wrote to everyone.

We read all of our articles collectively every other week for the entire class. "All of you should be familiar with what your fellow colleagues are writing," Mr. Cannon said.

"How would we even do that?" Denton asks.

"That's what I'm asking you."

Jeanna asks, "Won't we get in trouble?"

"I'm not worried about that right now."

"It is actual news," Blane says.

"The question is: will you help me get this in the paper?" I ask. "I'm passing around a paper. Let me know if you want to help."

Mr. Cannon walks into the room, and we grow silent.

"Was there a secret meeting?" he asks.

A part of me wonders if he knows, but none of us say a word.

Unsurprisingly, Marcie and Jeanna, are out. Blane, Burley, and Denton are in. Of course, the last will be about as useful as walking around with a bag of my own feces.

After class, Blane talks to me in the hallway. "I have an idea of how we can go about this."

Chapter 68

Phase one of the plan involves sneaking into the school at night. Surprisingly, Blane knows a guy who knows a guy who can swipe the key for us. Once, he wrote an article about radios being stolen from cars at the Homecoming football game. Naturally, he assumed the school surveillance cam would provide evidence, but when he looked into it, it turned out there's only cameras for the staff parking lot.

The thieves got off and no one knows who took them.

He even followed this up by sneaking into the school and analyzing the surveillance equipment.

As if this wasn't contribution enough, Blane says he's familiar with the program to put the paper into the school from a flash drive. It goes from Word to this document program called Design something.

"What's the big plan?" Carmen asks as we all sit on her living room floor. Her lack of parental units is noticeable, mirroring my own.

Denton takes a hit from a blunt, exhibiting his poor stoner mannerisms. As normal, he hogs the blunt, taking extra hits instead of the courtesy hit or two and passing it.

"Puff-puff-pass," I say.

He hands me the blunt.

The hope is that the THC coursing through our system will help conjure up a logical plan. It's more of a concept that *should* work, and we have all of the elements here; we just need to piece them together.

I attempt to pass the blunt to Blane, but he grimaces and shakes his head.

"Blane gets the key tomorrow then we meet in the parking lot where we know there's not a camera and upload the story," Carmen says. "Simple, right?"

"But if there are other security cameras?" I ask, looking at Blane.

"I assure you, as long as we enter from the *student* parking lot it will work," Blane says. "We just can't enter from the staff parking lot."

Carmen leans into me, "Maybe if I'd been easier we wouldn't need all of the planning."

"Sometimes life needs more than sheer luck. As that doesn't always work. Besides, what you tried earlier didn't work."

Taking another deep hit of the blunt doesn't alleviate any of the tension.

Carmen takes a hit of the blunt and as usual doesn't cough.

"Brandon. I know that guy that does the computer stuff," Denton says.

"It's not that simple," Carmen says. "We already talked to him."

"Alright, Blane will get the key from his friend and meet us in the parking lot of the church across the street," I say. "That way it won't alert suspicion by having cars in the school parking lot. We make sure to enter the school from the student parking lot where there are ironically no cameras."

Blane gives a thumbs up.

"Carmen enters the parking lot first, making sure nobody is there. Then she gives us the go ahead via walkie-talkie. Then, we make our way through the school to the technology lab. We leave Carmen to watch the door and alert us if anybody is coming."

It's all coming together. Who says marijuana doesn't solve problems?

"Let the girl be the lookout," Carmen says, rolling her eyes.

I frown at her, and she shrugs.

"And Denton ..."

He raises his eyebrows; his eyes are bloodshot.

"You just come with me and try not to bump into anything."

"And then what about the computer?" Carmen asks.

"I've seen how Brandon sets up the paper before. I can do it," Blane says. He loves the idea of any true news and probably has a boner right now.

"I told you before I know the guy that—"

"So the plan is set," I cut Denton off.

We agree to wear all black because it feels right.

We meet in the church parking lot for our co-op secret mission. Operation Freedom of Lakewood High Press. It's already dark out and it's not even late.

"You remember the walkie-talkie code, right?" I ask Carmen.

She rolls her eyes and exits the car, walking across the street to the school parking lot. Denton isn't here which may be for the best.

"What's your 20?" I ask into the walkie-talkie. "Over."

"My what?"

"Your 20 is your location," I inform her. "Over."

"It's all clear."

"And your 20 is? Over."

"In front of the door where I said I'd be." I can hear the annoyance in her voice. "Over," she says with enough venom to where I can feel the arm punch through the walkie-talkie.

"Copy, over."

Blane looks at me like I'm deranged. "We can literally *see* her from here."

The second we make it across the street and to the door, someone walks up behind us.

"Took you guys long enough." Denton says.

"We were supposed to meet at the church and in all black."

"I didn't have any," he says, pulling at his brown t-shirt. "But brown is close enough, right?"

This is a bad idea, we're all going to get expelled.

"The key?" I ask, looking at Blane.

He pulls it out, holding it up like a prize. He opens the door and we walk into the darkness. I've never seen the school this dark.

"Well, there's no turning back now," Burley says.

Even though we have all gone here for years now we question which way to turn down each hall.

We make it to the technology lab where the document design courses are held.

Blane flips on a computer. A screen with a username and password appears. Blane gets at it.

"My student ID isn't working." he says.

"What?"

He types in the box, but an error screen comes up. He makes several failed attempts.

"You don't know the password?" Burley asks.

"It doesn't let any student just log in. How would I know these computers are different than in the rest of the school?"

Our IDs let us log into any computer in the building, or at least that was the impression I was under as well.

"Probably because they don't want people screwing around with the paper like us," I say.

Denton leans over the computer. "It's not gonna work?" he asks. "I can type in my password?"

"I'm sure your password will be different." He fails to pick up on the sarcasm.

I rub the back of my neck. We hear the noise of footsteps behind us.

"What's going on guys?" Carmen asks from the doorway causing us all to jump and pretend we didn't.

"You're supposed to be lookout," I snap.

"You guys are taking forever."

"Why didn't you radio?"

"I forgot I had it."

She would not dub well as a secret agent.

"It's password protected," I say. "Apparently students can't log in."

We all look at each other like someone is going to have some epiphany, but no one does.

We hear another noise. Maybe we're imagining it.

Burley looks around frantically. "Let's get out of here."

We make our way back to the parking lot, defeated. Blake and Burley take off in one car. Carmen and I in another. Denton takes off in the car he parked in the *student* parking lot.

"At least we tried," I say on the drive back.

"All that for nothing."

Chapter 69

We're silent the next day and none of us discuss anything about the previous night. Burley and Blane nod at me as I walk by them.

Carmen and I are melancholy, standing by her locker after Physics. I can't say I absorbed anything that was talked about during class.

"I guess we're out of options," I say.

"We could have just printed it out and distributed it," Carmen says.

"That's something a loser would do," I point out. "We actually have a school paper. It seems like it's not coming from a legitimate source if we do that."

"But it would be better than nothing."

"It's all or nothing."

Denton walks up to us, appearing jovial.

"He said yes," Denton says.

"What are you talking about?" I ask.

"Brandon. He put the article in the paper."

"We already talked to him," Carmen dismisses him.

"Like I said, I know him, and we sometimes smoke pot after school," Denton says. "When I first moved back, he was the main person I'd blaze with after school. It's already done."

"How did you get Brandon to do it?" I ask.

"I offered him some pot," Denton says.

Talk about coming up big when least expected.

"He did it for pot but not for me?" Carmen asks, looking angry.

Now, it's my turn to smirk. "Maybe you're just not his type?"

"Can I borrow $10 for lunch?" Denton asks.

And this is the one time where I gladly oblige.

Chapter 70

Phase two of the plan involves waiting for the inevitable shitstorm that will follow ... I opt to avoid it at least temporarily.

"I think now might be a prime time to skip," I say.

"I thought skipping was frowned upon and you were devoted to your studies," Carmen teases.

"No, seriously. I don't want to be here when this all goes down."

We hang around with no intention of going to 5th or 6th hour. "Hey, can I get a copy?" I ask Tanya Larue as she walks with a stack of the *Lakewood Bi-Weekly*.

"Of course."

I flip to my article. It came out exactly as intended. While not a tremendously long article, it's weird knowing people will read it. And it's odd that less than 500 words of text can expose everything.

There are going to be repercussions," I say.

"Are you worried?" Carmen asks me.

I don't say anything.

"I'd never thought I'd see the day Mr. McCarthy was worried about an article he published."

"This time it's different."

We pause after exiting the door to the school's parking lot. No real plan in place.

"What do you want to do?" Carmen asks.

"I don't know. I guess enjoy the last real nights of freedom I have."

"It's not like they're going to lynch you."

"They just might. I've gotten so many warnings and Mr. Cannon seemed serious. He's never stopped me from publishing an article before."

"So serious." She looks at the ground as we walk.

We're walking through the school parking lot and the parking lot Nazi eyes us suspiciously.

"What's our plan?" I ask.

"We have to make your last nights of freedom worth it," she says.

We drive to Michigan City—which, in fact, is in Indiana, not Michigan—to catch a train to Chicago. Michigan City is janky as hell and does a disservice to anything labeled as "Michigan." Rundown houses and junkyard cars fill the city.

Carmen drives because apparently she knows the way. And it's supposed to be some type of "surprise."

"Are you taking me to be killed?" I ask.

"It's not that bad," Carmen says. "I have a few cousins who live here."

Phone calls are made. I call my dad and tell him I'm staying at Carl Denton's house overnight. Carmen makes a similar phone call to her dad, reassuring her she's staying at Alexis' house. My dad doesn't say much.

"I don't see why we're doing this," I say.

"But you will see."

"Doubtful."

"You haven't even been out of the state, except on the trip with your mother," Carmen says. "It's time."

The train ride feels brief. Like I'm leaving all of the problems of Michigan behind. The article doesn't matter. But a tightness enters my stomach; I've never been outside of Michigan except when I was a kid.

"You're thinking about it," Carmen says.

The train is filled with passengers of different ages and races.

"No, I'm not."

Carmen looks at me. "It will be okay."

"I frankly don't know what you're referring to."

"Don't worry about the article right now."

After forever, we arrive. Carmen leads the way. "You have to see this," she says. "I've only seen it once before when I was a kid with my dad."

Chicago has *too* many people in it. There are too many buildings. But in a weird way we just blend into it all and are lost. Nobody questions us as we exit the train or asks us where we're going.

We're free.

Carmen grabs my hand and leads the way.

We eventually arrive at the John Hancock building. The fifth tallest building in the United States. When you look up you feel vertigo. It's dark and ominous.

"I don't know if I can do this."

Carmen grabs my hand.

"Why do we need to do this?"

My heart beats faster and sweat trickles down my neck and forehead. Everything I imagine about being in a new place doesn't feel the same.

"You need new experiences," Carmen says. She hugs me. She feels warm and it's like everything melts and things are exactly where they need to be. I could enjoy her scent for years.

We enter the lobby and get tickets. There's a line. Each second reminds me of how real it is.

When it's time to go to the elevator, I feel this sense of panic. I've never been in a tall building. Especially not a building this tall.

"It's okay," Carmen reassures me.

My ears pop as the elevator rises. We go higher and higher into the unknown.

Carmen grasps my hand.

We arrive and exit. It's just a room but with lookout windows throughout it. Each spot exhibits a display with a bunch of writing on it, and it reminds me of a museum.

Carmen sees me looking and says, "Don't pay attention to any of that. Just look. Feel. Experience."

She smiles and squeezes my hand harder.

And in this moment, everything is alright.

We arrive at a big window.

"Look," Carmen says.

The sun has set and it's dark out. I look out the window, and I see the lights of the city, like a cornfield ablaze. A million lights appear from every direction, and it goes on forever, as far as the eye can see. It's weird thinking about how big a place can be. How many stories it can hold. But this is our story and none of that matters.

"This is when I realized there's this entire life out there. Life existed beyond my shitty home."

In every direction I look there is nothing but light and the light continues infinitely.

We take the train ride back home and Carmen sleeps on my shoulder the majority of the way. I don't complain. She feels warm next to me, and I don't want this moment to end. She wakes up once and looks at me but drifts off again and I wonder what she's dreaming. If she's dreaming of me.

I want to know what she wants out of life and if I'll be a part of that life. But, I think it's best not to question everything. I enjoy having her next to me. Even though she starts to snore towards the end of it.

We drive back in a haze of tiredness.

Carmen makes me drive.

"Thank you," I say.

"I'm so tired," she says. "We're staying at Alexis' house tonight."

"Why?"

"Because."

"Such impeccable reasoning."

"Are you saying you don't want to sleep in the same bed as me?"

My interest is piqued and immediately my mind wanders. Thoughts of what color Carmen's bra is and feeling her breasts again. Kissing her pouty lips. Running my hands up her legs.

Alexis has a garage that dubs more as an extra room that her older brother used to sleep in.

"I'll take one for the team."

"You're so generous." She smirks through her tiredness. "I mean if you *have* to. I wouldn't want to force you or anything."

"You're making us move so fast."

She smiles.

"Cut the lights before we enter the driveway," Carmen instructs.

"Why?"

"Just do it. It's what everyone does this late."

I drive up in complete darkness.

When we get there Alexis greets us. "They won't notice. Just don't throw a crazy party."

"Otherwise the cops might show up again?"

Alexis looks at me unamused. "And wear protection."

"We're not doing anything."

"It's not up to me," Alexis says. "I just don't think the world is ready yet for little Carmens running around."

"If they'd be anything like Carmen then no," I quip.

"I'm not even going to respond to that." Carmen yawns.

Carmen grabs my arm. The room looks like I pictured it. A bed. I'm sure at one point there was a T.V. and a gaming system, but I imagine her older brother took all of that to college.

"I can sleep on the floor," I say.

"Why?"

"I'm not like that."

"Sleep in the bed with me," Carmen says. "I'll feel better if you do. Besides, I'd rather sleep in the same bed with someone I want to sleep with."

"Do you want me to sleep in my boxers?" I joke.

Carmen looks at me like she wants to punch me in a non-playful way. "Don't push it."

"I'm kidding."

"You can."

Nothing takes place, but in a weird way, it's nice just being next to her even though our bodies aren't touching. I debate trying to move closer to her, but I don't want to upset her and ruin the moment.

We lie on our sides facing each other.

Her breathing gets deeper. For a second, I watch her. Her eyes close. I try to take it all in. Her smell. How peaceful sleeping she looks.

We wake up at almost the same time in the morning.

"I have sex hair and we didn't even do anything," Carmen says. Her hair is an array of chunks sticking up in the back. I learned this term from her many months back.

"Good."

She looks at me with a look I'd describe as less than happy.

She drops me off by my car in the church parking lot. She hugs me and we part ways.

I walk inside my house, still aware of the shitstorm that will ensue, but it feels lighter somehow.

Chapter 71

Mr. Cannon stands outside the door before first hour. He informs me, Mr. Gensen and Principal Harris both want to talk to me, immediately. While talking to the administrator of discipline, Gensen, is never good, when both want to talk to you, it's *superbly* not good. In my educational career, I've yet to have the honor of being sought after to converse with both. Let alone, at the very start of the day.

"We're going to have to have a talk after this as well," Mr. Cannon says, his voice serious. No matter-of-fact-ness. No *this is just the way journalism goes sometimes* with a sad nod.

"Do you—"

He cuts me off. "Go and talk to both of them. Don't be surprised if I'm requested to make a visit after or during your meeting."

"But—"

"I'm not saying anything more."

I walk the walk of doom. Different than the other times I've done it. Before I felt a sense of vindication, like I knew for sure I was in the right. Or, if not, that I had done something comical worth the punishment. Maybe—I'll admit this one time—I overstepped by bounds.

Mostly throughout my academic career I've gotten detentions—at this point, to be honest, I've lost count but I'd estimate over 30—and a few of my offenses led to multiple detentions, but never suspension.

I wonder what Pops would say.

Normally, I wouldn't worry about this kind of stuff. As I've said before, I've *forged* his signature hundreds of times. It'll be kind of hard to fake a suspension. I guess I could *pretend* to go to school every morning and find stuff to do during the week. However, I'm sure this might warrant a phone call home.

Now, if I got expelled, I'd have to fake this for another year and two months then when Pops and Gramps want to show up to my graduation that'll be kind of hard to fake.

Both of them are waiting in Principal Harris' office. Gensen's wearing his normal cowboy boots but by the grave expression on his face it lacks the amusement it normally does. While I doubt anybody has ever seen Principal Harris smile in the history of his tenure—all eight magnificent years—his eyes look menacing.

"I take it you know why you're here, Mr. McCarthy," Principal Harris starts.

"I have ... an idea."

"We tried getting a hold of you Friday, as a matter of fact," Gensen interjects. "But it turned out somebody was absent for their last two hours of the day."

I look at the floor.

"We talked to Mr. Cannon, but he was unaware your article was printed in the paper. In fact, he told us he strictly told you *not* to print it," Principal Harris says. His eyes bear into me.

"He had nothing to do with this," I say.

"How did the article appear in the paper then if it wasn't supposed to?" Gensen asks.

This is where I could explain about attempting to pirate the press and how it was easier to sneak into the school than you'd think, the slight misunderstanding about the lock on the school computers, and at the end sheer luck from an unlikely source, but I opt for silence.

"What if I said I didn't know anything about how it got in the paper and had nothing to do with it?"

Both of them look at me like I tried to convince them the world is flat.

"I mean what *evidence* do you have?" I ask.

"For one, you wrote the article," Principal Harris says. "You can say somebody else wrote it and put your name on it, but we know this is your voice. At the very least you wrote the article and somebody published it in the school paper even though they weren't supposed to. I'm not saying you acted alone in the matter, but you had something to do with it."

I look around the room. My third strike.

"Maybe somebody stole it from me."

They both look at me, and I can tell their bullshit detectors are going off.

"You have to realize the repercussions for your actions," Principal Harris says. "Our school district holds a very important role in the community. We want to project an environment that's wholesome."

Meaning nobody who is transgender. Our squeaky-clean image in this white heterosexual community. How Harris wants everybody to view us. His "normal." Not reality. Not how the school actually is. *If you want to talk about drugs go to Muskegon, if you actually want to do drugs go to Lakewood High.*

"We don't want the negative attention of the press or the news. We want to be away from controversy."

"Must protect our good image," I blurt out, sarcastic.

Principal Harris glares at me; a weird type of smirk forms on Gensen's face.

"Must we remind you, Mr. McCarthy that this is not your first offense?" Gensen asks. "We've been far too lenient with you, against my better judgment."

"My memory is pretty crystal."

"Tell us," Gensen says. "We know you couldn't have acted alone in this. Who else was involved?"

This is the part where I could mention Carmen and everybody else, but the way I see it, I'm already going to get punished—whatever they have in mind for me. I'd only be handing out unnecessary detentions.

"We might be able to go easier on you if you told us who else is involved," Gensen says, trying to bait me.

Now my bullshit detector goes off.

"I acted alone." I'll never compromise Carmen or anybody who helped.

"We told you the consequences would only be worse the further you pushed your articles, Mr. McCarthy," Gensen says.

"Maybe if certain actions had been taken in the first place, we wouldn't be here right now," Principal Harris cuts in. "We don't need you to disgrace our school and we shouldn't have allowed such rants in the first place. You should be more than disappointed in yourself. Mr. Cannon should be disappointed in you. I can't even imagine how your father feels."

Principal Harris glares at me and I notice the blood vessels in his eyes flare.

"In light of these events, it's questionable if Mr. Cannon should even be teaching newspaper in the first place."

"This has nothing to do with him. He—

"Do not interrupt me ever again," Principal Harris says. "You've made a mess and this will be dealt with."

It's weird wanting to not be expelled and allowed in a place I don't want to go. I want to finish my sentence here, which surprises me.

"We want you to understand the full extent of the possible punishment, Mr. McCarthy," Gensen says. "We will ban you from writing any articles in the school newspaper for the rest of your high school career. You will no longer be allowed to take Journalism next year or the remainder of the semester."

"But you can't—"

"I'm afraid you don't understand," Mr. Gensen smiles, smugly. "We have full authority to disallow a student with a repeated history of disobeying the school's standards of articles to ever publish an article again."

"That's not fair."

"You have to understand the situation you have put us in, Mr. McCarthy," Gensen says. "This isn't a matter of pissing off a few parents." He pauses after saying the borderline swear-word "piss" and it's the first time I heard him say anything like this. "This is a widespread problem. Some of the damage may already be hard to reverse or do damage control on."

It's my turn to smile. "How much damage could one article in a student newspaper do?"

Mr. Gensen glares at me and doesn't smile. "Or we could go a different route and—"

Mrs. Penski, who operates the school's front desk, steps into the office.

All of us look up.

She looks at me heavy. "I just received a phone call from your father. Your grandfather is in the hospital. He's at Hackley Hospital with him now. He requests that you meet them there immediately."

"What happened? Why? He was fine last I saw him."

"I don't have details, but it is urgent."

Chapter 72

I ignore everything I've learned in driver's training as I speed to the hospital, cut cars off, run a red light, and definitely do not check my blind spots.

I don't understand; Gramps was perfectly fine last time.

Pops is in the waiting room and I rush towards him.

"What happened?" I ask.

"We're trying to figure that out."

"Well, it has to be something."

"I don't understand all of the medical terminology."

We go up to the room Gramps is in.

The smell of cleaners hit my nostrils, potent.

Upon entering the room, I notice how lifeless Gramp's body looks. His normally flush face looks paler and inanimate. His mouth closed tightly. I wonder what he thought before this happened and if he knew anything was wrong. Or if it all was like a flash and he became unconscious and immobile.

"Apparently he was having lunch with friends when it happened," Pops explains.

"He has friends?" I blurt out.

He gives me a strange look. "Maybe not many, but occasionally he does get out, which was lucky because if he was home alone who knows how long he could have been laying there."

"He was fine last time."

"I know."

I notice a speck blue on his blanket and wonder what it is.

A doctor enters the room and greets us.

"It appears he's had a Cerebrovascular accident," a doctor identified by his nametag as Dr. Hansen, speaks in code.

"What's that mean?"

"It means he had a stroke," I cut in before the doctor can answer.

"Is he ... will he be?"

"I can't predict how much damage there is, Mr. McCarthy, but it is serious." It takes a moment for me to realize Dr. Hansen is talking to Pops and not me.

"He'll wake up, right?" Pops asks.

"That's a possibility."

"And the other possibility?"

Dr. Hansen looks up from his clipboard, looking at me, and then my dad. "We are doing everything we can to make that possible."

My dad stares at Gramps and doesn't say anything for the longest time. What I'd give right now to have Gramps talk about how the Mexicans are taking all of our jobs.

My dad goes into a separate room with the doctor.

I look at my grandpa. He looks completely harmless laying there, almost peaceful, like he's not the type of person to dislike anybody.

When dad re-enters the room, his face lacks color and I notice wrinkle lines in his head I haven't noticed before.

"Let's go get some food," Pops says.

I look back at my grandpa. I know he'll wake up. Everything will go back to how it was before.

Chapter 73

Pops paces the floor like a madman after we get back from dinner. He barely touched a bite and rambled about Gramps. I mean it's not like I blame him ... It's not an ideal situation. And like a good son, I didn't bring up the potential trouble I could be in at school.

"He has to make it. He has to make it. He has to make it." Pops repeats this in a mantra.

"He will. People recover from things like this all the time. I'm sure the doctors are taking care of him."

It's not like he had a freak accident or was living a super unhealthy lifestyle. Then again, I think about how he watches hours of T.V., eats bologna sandwiches on only white bread, and I'll admit maybe it wasn't the healthiest.

The phone rings. My dad picks up the receiver. I know they're going to tell us Gramps is awake. We can go see him, but he may be a bit tired and take some time to recover and everything will be alright.

"No," Pops says. "No."

"What?"

He brushes me off with a wave of his hand.

"It can't be. There's no damn way. He wasn't that old." He's yelling into the phone.

He stands there holding the receiver and it feels like hours. Staring blankly. Finally, he says, "What do I do next?" I don't know if he's asking the person on the other end, himself, or a force beyond all of us.

He stands there and I don't need to hear the words to know what's happened.

Chapter 74

Everything costs money in life. Pops told me this before. I assumed this was only to drill into my brain the burden of living in modern society governed by monetary compensation—and a backhanded way of reminding me of the underlying emphasis I am his financial burden—but I never realized the full extent of this until today.

Dying costs money. I've heard that they charge quite a bit for delivering babies, all the hospital time, doctor's attention, but I never realized simply *dying* would be so expensive. I'm not including grandpa's hospital stay or any of that; this is on top of that. He could have went peacefully in his own home, sitting in that chair he loves so much, or in his sleep. A man can't even die without generating some sort of tab.

It makes me sick.

Pops and I are at System's Funeral home. There are about four different locations over town, and I suspect they're running a monopoly on the funeral business. And they'll never be out of business, because if it's one thing everybody has to do eventually after being born, it's die.

"I know this is a difficult time for you," the guy says, wearing a blue tie and a boring black suit. His hairline recedes and he doesn't look all that far off from kicking the bucket either.

"We have a brochure," he hands it to us. "We know you want to get the best you possibly could for your dad."

The rehearsed ingenuine way this comes out of his mouth makes me want to strangle him with his blue tie.

I look at the pamphlet with my dad. The prices are anything but cheap.

Blue Tie points to the brochure. "Many people go with this option: a nice mahogany casket. A very classy choice your father would appreciate."

"It's how much?" Pops asks.

"$10,000."

A person could buy a car for that.

"What else do you have?" Pops asks.

"We have this option as well. Great lining. Cherry wood."

"How much?"

"$8,000."

"Do you have any—I hate to say this—but cheaper coffins?"

We leafed through the booklet. Fancy coffins cost thousands upon thousands of dollars. When I looked, I didn't see anything less than $7,000.

"I think we're going to look somewhere else. Thank you for your time," Pops says and we turn to go.

"Wait," the funeral director says quickly. "We have another book. But don't you think your father would have wanted the best?"

"He won't know the difference." This sounds strangely cold coming from Pop's mouth.

They're playing on our goddamn emotions.

When the guy retreats to find the discounted coffins, my dad turns to me. "When I die, throw me in the river. Find the cheapest coffin you can. It's just a damn box in the ground. It could be plywood for all I care."

Chapter 75

My grandpa's visitation feels surreal. It's like how they look in the movies except worse and it drags on forever. It kind of resembles a movie, but it feels *off*.

A bunch of people show up who I don't know and constantly want to shake my hand and ask me how I'm doing. While I know I wasn't a big fan of Gramps, it's not like I'm doing *great* or having a stellar time, so it's kind of a dumb question to ask.

A guy in a big gray suit who I've never seen in my life stands in front of me.

"I remember when you were just a little guy," he says, putting his hand out like he's stroking an imaginary kid's head.

I don't say anything.

"I'm sure you don't remember me."

"I don't."

He converses with me, reminding me two more times I don't remember him. I nod, but my mind keeps thinking of the box lying up there. When I first entered, I caught a glimpse of the open coffin, Gramps' body looking like a wax exhibit in a museum. I glanced at it, but I didn't want to really *look* at it.

"It was nice seeing you," Gray Suit says.

"You too," I lie. He wanders off to harass somebody else.

Around us are a bunch of pictures. It's amazing how many pictures were in Gramps' basement and attic stored away. It was like he recorded every moment of his life with pictures. We put them all up on boards around the place. Black and white pictures decorate a couple of the boards. Other pictures show color.

Pictures spanned for his entire life. The earliest album from him as a four-year-old in black and white. Next to the picture is another younger boy, a girl who looks older than him, and two people who look like parents.

Pops is standing by me.

"Who are these people?" I ask.

"That's my dad standing with grandpa." I realize Pops means his grandpa when he says it, and it's weird thinking about him having a grandpa. "Your grandpa is standing with his brother and sister when he was younger and his parents." And it's weird thinking about how I don't even *know* my Gramps' name.

The picture looks like it was taken in the middle of the field in the country, and I imagine them having a house with nobody else around for miles and all the roads being dirt roads.

"He had a brother and a sister?"

"They're all dead now. He was the last one alive."

I knew my great-grandparents died before I was born. It's weird thinking about how everybody in the entire photo is no longer around, and they are just buried in the ground somewhere. Someday that's how all of us will be.

"How come he never talked about them?" I wonder out loud.

"It's how it goes. You remember and mention them occasionally but focus on the ones around you who are alive. They all went their separate ways, had families of their own, children, and then grandchildren."

It's weird imaging my grandpa before he had wrinkly skin, gray hair, and mostly sat in his chair spewing anger towards the racially changing neighborhood. Or hard to imagine him before his punctilious obsession with his yard.

When I think about it, I can see his whole life from when he was a child to where he lies forty feet away from me in his coffin. He once had dreams, family, a fully extended family. He was more than just a grandpa and it didn't encompass his whole life.

I make my way through all of the pictures twice. People come up to me and shake my hand. Friends of my dad that he hasn't seen in years. Friends of my grandpa. Gramps' church congregation. It almost makes it hard to imagine him as just some old guy sitting in a chair all day.

Chapter 76

I've never been to a funeral. Nobody I've been even remotely close to has died. Everyone greets each other, and there's a separate room where we can view my grandpa's corpse and say whatever we feel we need to in order to process the whole ordeal. It looks the same as yesterday and feels like yesterday.

Nothing anybody says makes any of this any better. They say things like, "He's in a better place now." Or, "He's watching over us."

While, frankly, I don't believe in any of that or see how lying in a room with people staring at your dead body makes any of this better, I remain quiet. A part of me wonders what his last thoughts were. Did he *know* he was dying and this was it? Did his life flash before his eyes?

Or was it just like he felt like he was going to take a nap and never woke up?

"I asked them to keep the service quick," Pops says. Whether it's because we don't do the whole church thing anymore or because he doesn't want to be here any longer than I do, I'm unsure.

Everybody wears their best.

It's my first time wearing a suit. Carmen helped me with the tie. Of course, she's here, even though I told her she didn't have to be, and it'd be a waste of time; she never even *met* my grandpa.

My grandpa is in a room before the service. I wonder if he would have preferred his funeral in a church or in the funeral home, but then a funeral seems kind of like a dumb thing to plan on account you won't be present at your own—aside from your dead body obviously. When I have my funeral, I want them to make it as quick as possible. Or I'll make it a game like a scavenger hunt or something. The main thing missing will be my dead body; they will have to find it in the end. If they fail to do this to meet certain time requirements, they'll have to start from the beginning until they get it exactly right.

The pastor arrives.

We put pictures in my grandpa's casket with him, pictures of me when I was little, or him with my dad, or him with his whole family while they were all alive. All of the other pictures still decorate the walls, reminding us of the life he lived.

I'm the last one in the room with him.

We had a little prayer party earlier where the pastor said a few words. I listened, but I didn't *feel* anything. People say you can just feel when the Lord enters you and all that, but I don't feel it.

Gramps still looks like a mannequin in a wax museum. Not even real. Nothing that was him is left in there.

"I know you can't hear me, Grandpa," I say. "But I just want to let you know I realize we didn't agree on everything. I'm sorry for all of the times I was shitty to you. I guess saying all this now doesn't change anything or make it better, but it probably wasn't easy for you, being the last person left in your family. For what it's worth, I love you. I'm sorry I didn't say it enough at the end and I hated visiting you so much. Maybe I shouldn't even say that in case you can hear me."

I touch his hand. It's cold and doesn't feel like much of a hand, more like wax.

"And God," I say. "Can you take it easy on him? If you're up there and all, you know? He had a rough life. I think he did the best he could."

For a second, I try to picture grandpa going up to Heaven and the conversation between him and God.

God would say, "Welcome to Heaven."

Gramps would say, "It's close to five. What are we having for dinner?"

God would say, "We have all the time in the world."

"There aren't any goddamn Mexicans in here, are there?"

A Black person walks by.

Gramps asks, "You let *him* in here?"

I picture God as a white man in a white robe with long hair and a big thick light brown beard—and I wonder why this is the societal image forced on us and why He can't be a woman or of a different race—despite being in the middle of the friggen desert with the sun beating down on him constantly. It'd be hard not to be hella tan.

But then, I realize, I'm thinking of Jesus. But he was made in "God's image."

"You guys have Jeopardy in here, right?" Gramps would ask. He'd insist on sitting in front of the T.V. in a big rocking chair.

I wonder after seeing all of the pictures, if he'd want to be the age he died at. And—theoretically speaking, as the entire highly fictional situation elicits improbability—what age he'd prefer to be in paradise. If it'd be in his teens or twenties, or older. Then, I wonder if that option is presented. It'd be weird seeing him as someone my age or a little older when I know him as "Gramps." And what about the people who die before the age they'd prefer to be at? Surely, an infant wouldn't want to stay three forever, or a baby wouldn't want to be a baby forever.

But, maybe, that's not how it all works.

"Wherever you are, I hope you're happy," I say, thinking of how weird it is to occupy space, being a person, being alive one second then the next it's nothing.

I doubt anyone hears my words, but I say them as a just-in-case sort of thing. I made an attempt to talk to the benevolent being in the clouds.

Then the casket is closed and it's time for the funeral.

"Why did you say it has to be closed casket?" I ask Pops.

"It just has to be."

"But why? It's not like he's been in a crazy accident." I've heard of accident or homicide victims being in a closed casket but not a regular person.

"Stop asking questions. You're no longer a child."

I drop it. Maybe it makes the service easier, somehow.

The whole funeral ceremony reminds me of church. They sing songs, and I attempt to mouth the words at first, but I can't read music notes. The pastor says words that are supposed to make us feel better about God and his Son and all that.

Then they do a reading from the book of Job of all books. The worst book in the Bible.

The truth is Job is a selfish asshole. Maybe that's the whole point of the story; you're only supposed to worship and care about God then you're good with Him. Family or friends don't have to matter and if they die you should be happy—as long as you like the jealous cloud man and his son that's all that matters.

I wish Job would have died to be perfectly honest with you. I don't care how much he loved his god. The guy was still a jerk at best. A spineless self-centered douchebag would be more accurate who only cared about *his* physical suffering and not about his family.

After the reading, more words are spoken and we sing more songs.

Next, we're supposed to carry his casket and put it in the back of the car.

Pops nods at me. A group of us do it. I've been elected to help carry his coffin.

It feels heavier, like more weight is attached to it than there should be. For a second, I'm worried we'll drop it and ruin everything. We walk slowly. Six of us. We slide it into the back of the car and it feels so permanent, so final. This is it.

Goodbye, grandpa.

I realize at this point I'm crying, and the tears are streaming down my face.

Chapter 77

Nobody tells you that when someone in your family dies you get back all of the gifts you gave them.

After the funeral, we go over to where Gramps lived—something weird putting in past tense now, but it's accurate. Carmen goes to her home and Pops and I arrive first.

"There's so much stuff I have to take care of," Pops says. He had been doing it all the past few days. First, getting the death certificate to make it "official," which is kind of weird if you really think about it.

The second we walk through the door, it doesn't feel right. Normally, Gramps would meet us at the door, or he'd be in the kitchen or in the living room watching T.V. But there's only silence. The place doesn't even *smell* like his house anymore.

More people arrive. Instead of an auction, people get to choose what items they want from the dead person and are strongly encouraged to take any gifts back they previously gave them.

We start in the kitchen.

"Does anybody want these?" Pops asks. A collection of glasses.

"I'll take them," Gray Suit says.

We continue this process through the other rooms of the house.

About five years ago, I got something for Gramps that was a hybrid between a blanket and a robe. He'd use it quite a bit actually. Pops picks it up and hands it to me.

"I don't want it."

"You will take it," Pops commands.

"What are you going to do about the house?" I ask, the thought never really occurred to me until that exact moment.

"We'll sell it eventually. Sooner rather than later."

I should have been relieved. This place where I listened to all his rants about "the gays" or Mexicans taking over the United States. Or how Black goalies shouldn't play in the NHL.

But I don't.

The dinosaurs will die out eventually. If they didn't in the past there's no way we'd have all the animals we have today, but maybe that doesn't make the process any easier?

This will mean no more playing Euchre with Gramps. No more going to his house again. I breathe deeply, trying to hold it all in. But it feels darker than I want it to. It's real but doesn't feel real.

At home Pops is drinking whiskey in his glass and he's refilled his glass a few times. I noticed he cried at Gramp's funeral but tried to hide it. He isn't crying now, but he's upset. The phone has been constantly ringing and it's the same goddamn conversation over and over again. "I'm so sorry for your loss." It's the obligatory line everyone says and it sounds like it's coming from a robot. It reminds me of how someone asks how you're doing without caring about the answer.

The phone rings again and it's some guy who we used to go to church with when we attended. "I'm sorry for your loss," he says. "I couldn't attend the funeral."

Like I care.

"Thanks," I say.

"How's your dad holding up?" I have no idea who this person is even though he said his name.

"He's handling it."

He blabs on until I interject, "I'm sorry. I have to go. I have explosive diarrhea."

Normally, I'd let my dad answer the phone, but I figure he could use a goddamn break.

I pour vodka out of a water bottle into a glass of Coke before I enter the room. You can have an alcoholic beverage in front of most adults and as long as it's disguised as a normal beverage, they won't notice the difference. With the state Pops is in, I'm not even remotely worried.

"Everybody is so fake," I say as I walk into the room.

"Did you ever think that maybe adults are just being polite?"

"It's a cop out—they're counterfeit people."

"Maybe they just don't want to tell you that life won't turn out how you think it will and everything turns to shit."

Normally, he doesn't say stuff like this. His eyes are bloodshot and he's swaying. I know he gets tipsy at times, but normally he's not *this* drunk.

"I never told you about what happened with your mother." He takes a gulp of whiskey; the intoxicating fumes almost make me feel buzzed.

He only told me she left. When asked to elaborate, he never did. No matter how hard I pressed him.

"You were only four," he says. "She started drinking ... heavily. By the time you were two, I'd come home and she'd be passed out on the couch while you were walking around the house. It came to the point I couldn't even trust her with you. I begged her, pleaded with her, to get cleaned up, but she wouldn't listen."

"Has she always been like this?" I ask, not knowing if I want to know the answer.

"No, she'd rarely drink before, only on special occasions. It was like something inside her just broke and I didn't know how to fix it. One day she was just gone. She left a note. I still have it."

"Where?"

As I said before, I've searched every square inch of this house.

He grabs his wallet. He pulls out a neatly folded piece of lined paper crinkled from age.

"I don't know if I want to see it," I say. So much for picturing her on a rescue mission, building homes in Africa. Or as a double agent in the secret service.

"I'll leave it here," he lifts up a bottle of vodka and puts it under. "You can read it if you ever choose to. If not, that's okay too. You've made it this long."

"Why not put it on the table or somewhere?"

"I know here you'll be able to find it."

I get up, wanting to be away from the room, the smell of the whiskey burns my nostrils. I want to be out of this house.

"By the way," Pops says when I'm at the stairwell. "Try not using the same bottle each time you swipe vodka from me. It tastes like water at this point. Also, Axes doesn't cover up the smell of pot as well as you think it does."

Chapter 78

"Dad," I say.

He's sitting on his bed, staring off. He looks at me.

"The trip to the East Coast. When we saw the ocean. With mom …"

He looks down.

And I know.

A story he told me my whole life. The one and only memory I have of my mother. Then only the mysteries.

He looks at me.

"It never happened, did it?"

He shakes his head and there are tears in his eyes. They're streaming down his cheeks. After what seems like minutes, he finally speaks, "I wanted you to have one good last memory of your mother."

"But it wasn't real."

"You asked so many questions when you were a kid," he says, wiping the tears from his eyes. "I didn't know what to say. How to answer your questions."

I've only seen my dad cry a handful of times. And never like *this*. Real tears. He'd always scoff anytime I'd cry as a kid and tell me I was being a baby.

"It's okay," I say. I sit next to him on the bed. I give him a hug even though we don't generally do the whole hugging thing. He cries more. "I know you did the best you could. The best you knew how."

My dad passes out shortly after.

It's weird how I used to think he had it all figured out. I mean I knew not *completely* everything, and it would have helped having an extra parental unit in the house, but maybe he didn't figure out as much as I originally thought?

I go to the liquor cabinet and open the letter. It feels soft from years of being in my dad's wallet. It's written on a sheet of regular lined paper, and I think about how it's been 12 years since my mom wrote it.

It's addressed to my dad.

David,

I'm sorry. I know that isn't enough.

I can't do this anymore. I don't know how to help myself. I don't know what's wrong with me. It's like all I wanted my whole life was to be a mother and have a kid. I thought that would make me happy. It was what I always wanted.

It's not enough anymore. I think constantly about the life I wish I had now. I want to go to parties, and to live in a big city, live a life full of excitement. The thought of leaving constantly crosses my mind to the point it's inbearable.

I don't know where I'm going to go or what I'm going to do. I know I can't stay here anymore.

Take care,

Elissa.

Setting down the letter, I'm first disappointed my mom isn't a very good writer. Secondly, I notice the misspelling of the word "unbearable." English clearly wasn't her strong suit. Third, I truly know how Carmen feels about having a mom who wishes she never had her.

Chapter 79

It's time for sentencing. I've been absent for school for the past week. Not like it hasn't been gnawing on my mind, but now it feels real.

It's the longest walk of my life as I'm expectedly called down to the office the first hour of my first day back. Like a prisoner walking from death row to be electrocuted, I debate asking if I can at least get a last meal.

I think I'd opt for a crunch wrap supreme.

While all of those other times walking to the office, I felt a little nervous and filled with dread, this time I know it's for real. I may never write again for the school paper, be able to conduct interviews, be in Mr. Cannon's class. I might not be able to graduate—which in a way would be a goddamn relief not having to step foot in this school again—and that thought makes me a little bit sad. Only one more year to go.

I arrive at the office door and take a deep breath.

Mr. Gensen and Principal Harris are waiting for me.

"We are sorry to hear about your loss," Mr. Gensen says. "However, it does not excuse what you did, and you need to understand there are consequences."

For every action there is an equal and opposite reaction.

Mr. Gensen clears his throat, less for dramatic effect, than to clear the phlegm.

"We've decided to ban you from any extra-curricular activities, you are no longer allowed to participate in the newspaper in any way nor take classes in journalism or any related field, you will serve two weeks of detention, and be suspended for one week."

Kind of what I thought, but it still feels like all the air has been sucked out of my lungs.

"You are not a first-time offender, Mr. McCarthy."

I nod.

Principal Harris looks at Mr. Gensen. "And," Principal Harris says, "You will issue a letter of apology to the school about how irresponsible your article was and how inaccurate it is. The paper will retract everything you said, but we want everyone in the school to hear it directly from you."

"You can't—"

"If you refuse to write the letter or disobey any parts of this punishment, we will have no choice but to expel you from school."

"I will not write a letter saying it's false," I say.

"Mr. McCarthy, think about graduating," Mr. Gensen says.

"That's bullshit," I say.

"As of this moment you are permanently expelled from Lakewood High School."

Chapter 80

The phone rings again. I want to slam my head into the table every time the receiver rings. Sometimes I let dad answer the calls or hand the phone off to him, but I've still been answering the majority of the calls. I debate disconnecting the phone.

"May I speak to the student who published the article in the school paper from Lakewood High titled *Snow Coming Election Fruad?*" A female voice asks.

"Speaking."

"This is Linda Nuttle from ABC looking to speak with you about the article."

"ABC from the ..."

"From the news, the local branch. We air every night at 6pm."

"Like on the T.V.?" I ask, regretting sounding like a moron the second it comes out of my mouth.

"Yes, on the T.V. We could sit down to talk, possibly meet at your school?"

"I've been expelled," I inform her.

"Really?"

I don't feel like going into all of the details and if I should. I guess a part of me—even though I know it's kind of hopeless—hopes they will change their mind.

"That seems a bit extreme for someone exercising their freedom of press about an important issue."

"The administration didn't seem to think so."

"Perhaps we can talk about this in person."

"In front of the camera?" I guess, if I'm being honest, I'm not all that thrilled about the idea of being in front of a camera.

"Yes."

"I don't want to be on T.V."

"But think of all the good it could do by letting the public know the truth. You can hold the school accountable."

I guess since I'm expelled and all, it would be nice to get the administration back a little. I can imagine Mr. Gensen's jaw drop and see Principal Harris getting red in the face already as they sit in their homes watching it on T.V.

"Okay, I'll do it."

We set up a time to meet.

When I first told Pops about the expulsion, he kind of flipped his shit.

"What do you mean expelled?"

"Exactly how it sounds. I'm not allowed to ever come back, and I'm banned for life."

"I should have never let you get away with all of this shit. The alcohol. The pot. Your life is going downhill. I should have put an end to it right away."

I didn't know what to say.

"If you wouldn't have been so stupid, you wouldn't be in this situation."

I remained uncharacteristically quiet, figuring it was best to let him get it all out.

"They didn't give you any warnings?"

I thought then maybe wasn't exactly the best time to mention forging his signature on numerous detention slips or my two previous warning about my articles.

"Can you at least let me explain?"

I walked him through the whole Avery thing. The article I wrote. Sneaking it into the paper.

"All this over an article?" he said, finally calming down a bit.

"All of this is over the truth."

We didn't talk for the remainder of the day. This was two days ago. Now we're sitting in front of the T.V. It's nighttime and the news is on. I wait in anticipation, but don't expect them to say anything until after my interview.

"At Lakewood High a student has recently been suspended for publishing an article about how a transgender student, Avery Bowen, was denied the title of Snow Coming King by the school's administration," the woman, Linda Nuttle, who I talked to on the phone is standing in front of our high school.

"Avery has declined to comment but we will speak with the student who wrote the article."

The title under the story reads: Transgender Controversy?

"This poses the question of what are student's rights and how do schools protect those rights."

The camera goes out and they're back to the weather.

Pops look at me. "Looks like the school is in a predicament."

"The news want me to do an interview."
He looks at me. "Are you going to do it?"

"I agreed to but don't know if I should follow through with it."

"If you pushed it this far, you might as well finish it."

"I didn't mean to make a shitstorm and cause all this mess. I didn't—"

He hushes me. "Sometimes you have to stick up for what's right and for that I'm proud of you."

Chapter 81

The next day Pops informs me, "You have a visitor."

Carmen stands by the door.

"I'm sorry," she says before I can even say "hey."

"For what?"

"Everything. I pushed you. I heard you were expelled."

"That part's true."

I lead her to my room. A part of me wonders if Pops is going to have a hemorrhoid about it, but he doesn't say anything, only gives me a suspicious glance.

"Wow, look at you," Carmen says, glancing around the room. "Somebody is all neat and tidy."

"I've had a lot of time."

"I'm proud of you," she says, mockingly.

After a brief moment of silence she asks, "How are you doing?" I can tell she means it and isn't just asking like a person does who doesn't even wait to hear the answer.

"I know how you feel," I say.

"About?"

I show her the letter. I feel my chest convulse. No words can even come out. *It's not enough anymore.*

I'm not enough. Even though I was only a kid.

I think constantly about the life I wish I had now.

A life without me. I was a burden.

Carmen unfolds it, reading it. She lets out a breath.

I want to go to parties, and to live in a big city, live a life full of excitement. The thought of leaving constantly crosses my mind to the point it's inbearable.

None of this was what my mom wanted. She didn't even want to get to know me.

I realize I'm crying. I should have never read the goddamn letter. I was better off not knowing. Maybe sometimes imagining is better than reality. What we shape in our minds is greater than the truth.

She hugs me. It's one of those deep hugs that should be awkwardly long but isn't and I take her scent in, feel her hair, and I feel better. "I know I can't fix everything," she says, pressed into my chest.

"How'd you hear I was expelled?" I ask.

"Everybody knows," she says, looking at me. "Is that really what's important right now?"

Nothing feels important right now. After an even longer time, I ask, "How'd they find out?"

"I don't know. I didn't think you'd friggen get expelled though. Maybe in some trouble and I would be too."

"I'm not a snitch," I say. "They wanted me to say who was involved and they'd go lighter on my sentencing if I said, but I didn't. But what did me in was they wanted me to write a letter saying how everything in the article was false."

She looks at me, really looks at me and I think it's the longest we've held eye contact. I can see the sharp blue in her eyes and beneath it a hint of green.

She kisses me on the cheek. Her lips are warm and soft and take me by surprise.

"I'm sorry. I didn't know it would end like this."

"What have people been saying about the article?"

"Everybody is talking about it non-stop. Faculty hasn't said much but I feel like they were told not to. But everybody knows about it. It was on the news."

"I saw. They actually want to interview me about it."

"Are you going to do it?"

"I mean I'm already expelled. Not like they can kick me out again."

After Carmen leaves, I make a phone call that I need to make before I can do the interview.

Chapter 82

The phone rings yet *again*, this time I recognize the voice on the receiver. I can almost smell the leather cowboy boots.

"Mr. McCarthy, am I speaking with junior or senior?"

"Junior," I laugh. "What do you want?"

"This is—"

"I know who this is," I cut him off. "What do you want?"

"Principal Harris and I would like to invite you to have a meeting in my office tomorrow morning."

"I'm no longer allowed on school premises. Are you going to try to expel me *again*?"

"It's nothing like that. We want to talk about possible action to reverse your expulsion."

"That seems like a quick change of heart."

"Believe me, we have a tough job, Mr. McCarthy. We felt maybe we made too rash of a decision by expelling you, and we can work together to come to a reasonable agreement."

"What would that agreement be?"

"We want to talk about this in person with you. First thing tomorrow morning."

It dawns on me. The local news.

I walk into the living room and see the national news playing. "Transgender Student: Discrimination at School Dance?"

The national news.

Pops looks at me as I hold the receiver.

"I ..."

"It will be in both our best interest. I expect to see you first thing in the morning."

I hang up.

Pops asks, "Who was that?"

"The superintendent in my school."

"What'd he want?"

"To speak with me first thing in the morning."

"They know what a shitstorm this is." If I didn't know any better, I'd swear he's smirking.

"What do I do?"

"You play hard ball and play your cards right. Don't give into their every little demand." It's weird hearing him say this, but it makes sense.

"How can I do that?"

Pops smiles with a look I haven't quite seen from him before. I can almost see him protesting for equal rights back in the day and joining in marches. I think about how he stood up to Gramps. Maybe I don't know him as well as I think I do.

I make my way to the office yet *again*. It's weird this time because I realize there's not anything more they can do to me. It's not like they can expel me a second time, and since I'm technically no longer a student at Lakewood High, it's not like they hold much leverage.

I enter the office and Gensen is sitting at his desk with Principal Harris. To my surprise Mr. Cannon is in the office as well.

"Have a seat, Mr. McCarthy," Gensen says. Both Mr. Gensen and Principal Harris glare at me.

"I'd love to."

A strange calm washes over me.

"As you may know, we've dealt with a slight backlash from the news," Principal Harris begins. "We thought maybe we could come to a mutual agreement." The words sound like they are painful coming out of his mouth.

I don't say anything.

"We can reverse your expulsion under certain conditions."

Everybody looks at me.

After what feels like forever, I say, "I'm listening ..."

"We can agree to lighter terms depending on how the current situation is handled," Principal Harris says. His face is a deeper shade of red than I've ever seen, and I swear one of the veins in his head is going to pop.

"What exactly are you saying?" I need to be careful not to compromise too much, according to my dad. I have more leverage here than I think.

"What we are saying, Mr. McCarthy, is maybe it's in your best interest to not talk to the local media," Mr. Gensen says, not smiling and gritting his teeth.

"What do I have to lose? I'm already kicked out of school."

"You have a lot to gain by considering our offer."

"What's your offer?"

A part of me wants to tear the whole school down. I want to tarnish the entire school's image. I want to expose the truth and to reveal it all for what it is.

Mr. Gensen hesitates and takes a deep breath. "We'd remove your expulsion. We would ask you to write a letter to retract everything you said and that'd be it."

The words sound painful coming out of his mouth.

"I'm not going to retract anything," I say, slowly. "However, I can understand if I don't talk to certain parties, it might be in your best interest. If certain discriminations didn't come to even more light."

Mr. Cannon smiles.

"Are you threatening us?" Gensen asks. To say he looks more pissed than I've ever seen him would be the greatest understatement of the 21st century.

"I'm not threatening anybody." The same calm washes over me. "But I'm saying if certain parties learned how Lakewood High stands on certain issues it may become more of a PR issue than it already has."

Principal Harris and Mr. Gensen look at me. They don't say anything for what feels like an hour.

"We will remove the expulsion if you don't talk to the media," Principal Harris finally says.

"And?" Mr. Cannon asks, looking like he's repressing a smile.

"We will not pursue anything further," Principal Harris says. "We would like it if you'd follow up with some kind of letter in the newspaper. Maybe you don't need to *retract* anything, but something to clear the air. We will not ban you from publishing anything further in the newspaper. Please keep our interests in mind."

"I can agree to those terms. When will my expulsion be lifted?"

"Immediately, starting now."

And like that it's a done deal.

Chapter 83

When I enter third hour Physics, it's in the middle of class. Everybody stares at me like I'm Jesus coming back from the dead.

Carmen gets up and hugs me.

"What happened?"

"They lifted my expulsion."

"What? How?"

The whole class continues to stare at me and even Mr. West stops teaching.

"We will talk about this later. I'm sorry for disturbing class," I say.

"I didn't expect to see you again, Mr. McCarthy," Mr. West says.

"They lifted my expulsion this morning," I say loudly so the whole class can hear me. I don't elaborate.

Carmen immediately follows me after class.

"You're kind of following me around like a lost puppy," I say.

"Be quiet."

I don't say anything.

"Tell me what happened," she demands.

"You just told me to be quiet."

"Tell me." She pouts.

"Let's just say the school didn't want me to talk to certain parties about what happened," I say. "For my cooperation in not talking to the media, they have lifted my expulsion, and the only thing they want me to do is write some kind of letter in the paper."

"Do you have to say everything in the article was false?"

"They said I don't even have to write a letter of apology, but they'd like if I did."

"Are you going to be able to write more in the future?"

"Yes."

Avery walks to my locker. "The media is still hounding me."

"I didn't follow through on the interview, just like I told you."

"Thank God. I think this all went too far. I'm thankful you wrote the article and you stood up for me, but I don't like this. They're non-stop calling my house, asking me to do interviews from all over the place. I just want to be left alone."

"I never meant for any of this to happen …"

"I know."

Avery gives me a hug. "You helped in lots of ways."

Chapter 84

I bring my "letter of apology" to Mr. Cannon.

He starts reading it as I stand by his desk. He lets out a slight sigh and takes a sip of his coffee. Looking up at me he says, "Do you really want me to print this?"

Without hesitation, I say, "Yes."

"I don't know how the administration will feel about this one, but this time I have your back."

And here it is:

Everyone wants to shape the world they see around you and make you think it is something it is not. I want to start by saying I am sorry for all of the trouble my article caused. I published it without the school's consent and for that I regret it. Anytime you ignore your superior and their boss it does not lead to good outcomes I have found out.

But I would like to say, I have also realized what journalism truly is. It is not about writing what you're told. It is not about restricting yourself or being safe.

It is about seeking the truth.

Sometimes this goes awry, and it is hard to know what the right thing to do is. But it is imperative to seek this truth. Expose the lies. Push the boundaries. I have realized I crossed boundaries and did not always think about what was best for everybody involved.

I hope to always pursue justice. I do not know the school's process for determining Snow Coming King and Queen exactly, and I don't know for sure that the results were truly tampered with. I do hope that in the future there is not any reasonable debate about that. I am sorry for putting the school's golden reputation on the line, for causing discomfort to Avery Bowen, and for anybody I have hurt along the way.

You do not need to accept this letter. I am starting to realize it is not much of an apology. Realize that this is not the 1950's. The world is a different place, constantly changing. All I ask is that you accept those around you, treat them better, be better. There is already enough hatred, misunderstanding, and callous feelings in the world. Let's not add to this. Everything is constantly changing.

And I am too.

Chapter 85

We decided to go bowling instead of going to the Snow Coming Dance. Word on the street is most of the student body is boycotting the entire dance.

Principal Harris made an announcement the day after I came back that for future years, they will consider any two candidates from the same grade regardless of gender. It's a small win, but a win, nonetheless.

Avery, Carmen, Dustin, Benson, and I are bowling in one lane.

Others are taking up three more lanes. The whole newspaper crew, minus Mr. Cannon, is here.

I'm proud of the turnout.

"Who's going to win?" Avery asks.

"We're in competition?" I ask.

"If we don't have some kind, then it's no fun," Benson says.

"Are you two actually getting along?" I ask.

Avery shrugs and Benson says out loud, "Avery is actually really cool."

We proceed to bowl. I do terribly and have another "emasculating" performance. Carmen bowls amazingly, of course, getting strikes and spares, keeping us in the game.

"Do you think anyone actually went to the dance?" I leave it out there, curious.

Carmen shrugs. "From the people I talked to, most of them probably didn't. I'm sure some still went."

I'm not sure if this is a victory.

When we take a break Carmen and I are alone. She looks at me hard, pondering something. "Why didn't you do the interview?"

"I told you."

"No, really." Her eyes pierce through me. "You would have done it, regardless of being expelled for life."

"I told you. I wanted to graduate. Be a good student."

Her stare bears into me. "Don't lie to me. What happened?"

"Avery told me not to do the interview. I called him after you visited me. We talked about it. I realized that it shouldn't be up to me to do it. This isn't about me, and I probably shouldn't have been his spokesperson this entire time. You realize I didn't even ask him about the article I wrote after the first one?"

Avery admitted that he didn't even want the title of King but only wanted to get people thinking. He never expected to win or even come close to it.

Carmen sighs. "That makes sense."

I wasn't a responsible journalist.

"I don't regret sticking up for what was right, but it made Avery miserable."

For the second game of bowling, we decide not to take it seriously. We invent rules. The first frame we bowl with the opposite hand. The next we do granny-style.

Thirdly, we have to throw the ball between our legs. The next we do a spin move. And on it goes. Nobody does well and the score doesn't really matter at the end because all of us are laughing so hard.

"This is my type of bowling," I proclaim.

"I always like it when you don't take yourself too seriously," Carmen agrees. She kind of leans into me.

We spike our pop with vodka that somebody brought. We're very lowkey about it. Although Pops has me thinking maybe I'm not always as smooth as I think. Some people smoke cigarettes, and as Avery says, they never bother to card us.

In the parking lot we pass around a few joints. All of us get pretty lit. All in all, it's a good night and I can't complain.

Chapter 86

She's there again. By the door. Peering out into the vastness that's been taken from her—maybe partly from good intentions, maybe partly from the desire to have something else count on you. Winona watches the birds she once chased behind glass. She witnesses the animals moving around; she once was a part of their habitat, roaming free.

She looks up at me with her big eyes and I know.

"Meow!" She lets out a meow like I've never heard before, a calling, a beckoning to be released from this sentence imposed on her. One she took no part in. Humans always claim they know best. Strict boundaries are best. But I know by now that's not the case—it leads to control of the mind. It leads to denying what's right and what's right in front of your eyes.

I open the door.

"It'll be okay, girl. You'll find your way."

She pauses, looking at me.

I think we have a moment of understanding.

And she's off. Out into the unknown. Out to make her own freedom. To not be burdened by our restraints. To not have this crazy man with abandonment issues harassing her. She's free. To be herself. To be what she was before us. And I'd like to think a part of her will remember us, and that we made her life better, but I know the outcome which has to occur.

Her freedom.

I can't deny it.

Chapter 87

Carmen called me and confirmed almost nobody showed up at the Snow Coming dance. They even ended it early because of the turnout. Carmen then told me to come to her house. When I asked why she only said, "You need to come."

"That sounds like an order."

"It is."

I'm a sucker, willing to come on her command.

"Don't worry. Nobody will be home for at least an hour," Carmen says, meeting me at the door.

"What's that mean?"

"I tease you too much. I want to pay you for all your efforts." She smiles at me. I have a vague premonition of what she means, but I part of me doesn't believe it.

"I don't require compensation."

"I want to."

"Want to what?"

"I'll show you." She looks at me in almost a new way I haven't seen her look at me before. I want to say with longing, but I'm not sure if that's accurate.

She leads me into the basement. We sit on the couch—the same one we held hands on—and she pushes me down, kneeling in front of me. She looks me dead in the eye. Those eyes that hold the weight of the universe.

"You don't have to," I say. "Spending more time with you was honestly enough of a reward for me." Which I realize is true.

"Aww, now you've gotten sweet all of a sudden?" Carmen smirks.

She reaches for the button on my pants. She unbuttons them.

"I want to do it." She pulls a strand of her hair back. "I've worked up the courage for it."

"You really don't have to," I say, pausing, thinking about what she told me. "I'm not the type of guy that forces girls to give them blow jobs."

"It's not like I'm a child anymore. I'm doing it."

She reaches for my zipper. "No kiss first?" I ask.

"No. Wouldn't you rather say you've had your first blow job before your first kiss?" She smiles. "Sounds like something worthy of sharing in the locker room."

And this is where I'll fade out and not share any of the details for Carmen's privacy. But if I was asked, I would say that when people talk about all of the wonders of the world, they fail to mention their first blow job. If I was pressed in a locker room to say anything, I wouldn't because I don't want people to talk about Carmen like she's just a "slut" or like she's easy. If I was forced to share details about the experience, I would admit that no teeth were used during the endeavor and that to date it was the best forty-five seconds of my life.

About the Author

Craig Miller

Craig Miller has a bachelor's degree in professional writing with an emphasis in journalism. He has written and edited for numerous publications in the realms of aviation, law, and women's health. He has worked for 6 years as an ESL teacher for QKids. This is his first novel.

www.ingramcontent.com/pod-product-compliance
Lightning Source LLC
LaVergne TN
LVHW091711070526
838199LV00050B/2345